PRIVATE WOJTEK - SOLDIER BEAR

PRIVATE WOJTEK - SOLDIER BEAR

Krystyna Mikula-Deegan

Copyright © 2011 Krystyna Mikula-Deegan

The moral right of the author has been asserted.

Apart from any fair dealing for the purposes of research or private study, or criticism or review, as permitted under the Copyright, Designs and Patents Act 1988, this publication may only be reproduced, stored or transmitted, in any form or by any means, with the prior permission in writing of the publishers, or in the case of reprographic reproduction in accordance with the terms of licences issued by the Copyright Licensing Agency. Enquiries concerning reproduction outside those terms should be sent to the publishers.

Matador
5 Weir Road
Kibworth Beauchamp
Leicester LE8 0LQ, UK
Tel: (+44) 116 279 2299
Fax: (+44) 116 279 2277
Email: books@troubador.co.uk
Web: www.troubador.co.uk/matador

ISBN 978 1780880 037
British Library Cataloguing in Publication Data.
A catalogue record for this book is available from the British Library.

Typeset in 11pt StempelGaramondRoman by Troubador Publishing Ltd, Leicester, UK

Matador is an imprint of Troubador Publishing Ltd

Printed and bound in the UK by TJ International, Padstow, Cornwall

MIX
Paper from responsible sources
FSC® C013056

This book is dedicated to all those who experienced sacrifice and suffering during the Second World War; in particular the soldiers of the Polish 2nd Corps and 22nd Company (Artillery) and their families, including of course, Private Wojtek, the Soldier Bear.

ACKNOWLEDGEMENTS

I am indebted to my lovely mother, Janina Mikula, for her help in providing historical facts in detail, including her own experiences and those related to her as a young girl by her older brother Emil, a veteran of the 22nd. Company.

I would like to thank The Polish Institute And Sikorski Museum in London for their kind permission to use archive photographs of Wojtek and other soldiers.

In addition, I am grateful to Edinburgh Zoo for their help and co-operation.

Lucyna and Tadek, your input is much appreciated. I know you'll feel part of the story.

Last but not least, thanks to Pete, Leo, 'the boys' and Zorro.

Tomek and Marek, this is part of your history.

CONTENTS

Chapter 1 – Remembering the hero   1

Chapter 2 – From a frozen wasteland to the heat of the Middle East and Wojtek's Country   6

Chapter 3 – Meeting Wojtek   9

Chapter 4 – Raising Wojtek   19

Chapter 5 – Wojtek gets stuck in a tree and other adventures   22

Chapter 6 – Water baby Wojtek and the spy   32

Chapter7 – Wojtek has an eye for the girls   35

Chapter 8 – Empathy and cigarettes   39

Chapter 9 – We receive our orders and Wojtek is officially enlisted   48

Chapter 10   Operation Diadem   51

Chapter 11 – Holiday in Italy   63

Chapter 12 – New beginnings   70

Chapter 13 – *What* did you say?   78

Chapter 14 – Winfield Winter Wonderland   83

Chapter 15 – Drinking, Dancing, Romancing   87

Chapter 16 – Attitudes   97

Chapter 17 – Demobbed and in a dilemma about Wojtek   101

Chapter 18 – Goodbye Wojtek   105

Chapter 19 – Where is Peter?   111

Chapter 20 – Wojtek adapts to his new home   113

Chapter 21 – Wojtek finally accepts his new home   123

Chapter 22 – The sands of time   129

Chapter23 – Honouring ours   138

CHAPTER 1

Remembering the hero

My dear Wojtek, if you could only see how loved you still are and all the important dignitaries who have joined us, along with your old Polish friends, in remembering your antics and bravery during that terrible war.

But then, you always loved being a celebrity didn't you, you adorable old rascal? The horrors of battle seem such a long time ago now, out here in the bright autumn sunshine pouring out its warmth on this historic, elegant city of Edinburgh, through the chilly air signalling the approaching coldest season. What a long way we travelled. Now we are here at a magnificent monument erected especially for you, our hero, friend, brother; our much loved, special bear.

Yes, Wojtek was indeed a bear, a huge Persian brown bear to be precise, but one like no other in history so far as I am aware, for he was actually a soldier like the rest of us and became known as Private Wojtek (pronounced Voytek). I believe his story of love, friendship, bravery, humour and duty; of a bear with the heart and spirit of a man should be made known. I believe the hand of God sent you to us just when we needed you most, amidst the crippling suffering of war.

As I stand in front of your impressive bronze statue, which by the way depicts you sitting next to your beloved handler and our revered Lance Corporal Peter Prendys, I look around at our now aged comrades gathered here with me defying the cold, proudly standing erect; wrinkled hands firmly clutching standards bearing the red and white colours of Poland flapping gently above them in the calm breeze. Their dark suits decorated with hard earned war medals; berets perched perfectly on their snowy white heads. Traditional white and red sashes round their shoulders and fastened at the waist.

Just behind them are my old 'gang'. There's Irek, even now towering above the other veterans. He looks older, but still of an impressive build. His lustrous black hair though still plentiful, has turned grey and his brow more furrowed, but you could easily recognise him. His eyes are focussed on the monument. Was he reliving his happy wrestling matches with our hero?

Next to him is Stas, whose rather rotund figure gives the impression that he greatly enjoys his wife's meals. His round face shines in the sunlight, highlighting a surprisingly almost smooth complexion. Well, they do say that plump people tend to age better. He still wears glasses, but now they are of the more modern and expensive variety, with thin gold frames. A warm, grey, winter hat sits firmly and snugly right above his ears.

Then my gaze turns towards Henio, who has retained his thin, bony frame and facial features. I think he has probably aged the most. His wrinkles are more pronounced and his white hair has just about managed to keep a slight wave at the front, whilst the rest is short and his scalp almost transparent in places. His eyes reflect his feelings as openly as ever, though their shade of blue is slightly duller than I remember and dark shadows sit stubbornly under them. When did we all get so old?

As I stare at them in turn, I'm willing them to look up

at me. Just at that moment, Irek lifts his head and mouths a greeting. I acknowledge him with a nod. But I don't think the others have seen me yet. Or maybe Henio and Stas haven't recognised me? It's years since I saw those two, as they both decided to make their homes in Scotland after demobilisation. Irek and I were the only ones who moved miles away from Berwickshire, but close to each other south of the border. No, I'm sure I haven't changed *that* much, have I? I sigh deeply. They'll see me. We're all in our own little world of memories at the moment.

I feel tears welling up in my eyes for those who had been like our brothers during those difficult, dark days, but who hadn't made it to the end of the war, to freedom. It had been a time that was made so much more bearable (pardon the pun) by the gift of Wojtek amongst us. There is also sadness at how quickly the years have passed and the descent of handsome, youthful features into craggy, worn, lined faces. I look at the faces of other veterans from the 22nd Company (Artillery); at the haunted, distant look in their eyes. I'm sure that they too are quietly, solemnly, reminiscing about the ghosts of the past. I think of dear Peter and my wonderful Bolek. How I wish they were here.

The police commissioner's voice breaks into my thoughts. 'Wojtek was a true hero and we are here today to pay tribute to him and indeed all other Polish servicemen and women who helped Britain during the Second World War and thereby in doing so, sacrificed their lives. Wojtek's story is well known here to the good people of Edinburgh and I believe everyone should be aware of his important role in the war. There will be a short talk given by one of the soldiers who knew Wojtek well, along with some newsreel clips at the Council House reception in about half an hour.' A television crew are filming the proceedings and a young male reporter in a white trench coat is busily scribbling in his little black notebook. There is an explosion of flashes from cameras aimed at the assembled party of about a hundred people standing in front of the impressive memorial.

Scottish Members Of Parliament, trustees of the committee that had been elected to organise this event, including an elderly couple, who as youngsters had often visited Wojtek at Winfield Camp (where we Polish soldiers had to live when we first arrived on British soil after the war); a number of local residents and their children clap enthusiastically. Both the Polish and Scottish national anthems are sung with heartfelt gusto. Then the Polish community, some in traditional costume, sing 'Boze Cos Polske' a hymn of religious and patriotic significance. The old soldiers lower their flags as a salute to their comrades in arms, including the two represented by beautiful bronze figures standing motionless in front of us, frozen in expression and time.

As the crowd all slowly start to make their way out of the enclosure and down the sloping path bordering the worn grass that leads to the normality of the bustling High Street, just a short walk from the Council House, I turn round to my darling wife Krys. 'I'll meet you there dear.' She looks concerned. 'Are you sure Emil? I'll wait with you if you like.'

'It's alright Krys. I just need a few minutes on my own. I'll join you in a little while, I promise,' I say in a decisive tone, giving her a kiss on her cheek.

'Well…if you're sure……' she says with hesitation.

'Yes, I'll be fine. See you there.' I try to sound cheery and give her a reassuring smile.

'Right, but please come soon, ' she says, before following the procession. My comrades are all slowly walking together now right in the middle of a group of other senior citizens, so they can't get across to me at the moment. They're waving at me and call my name. I acknowledge them and shout, 'See you there!' though I'm not sure if they can hear me. Anyway, they'll see Krys at the Council House and she'll explain.

I watch until they're out of sight, then turn to contemplate the striking, stationary figures on the little raised platform in front of me. I stay for a little while longer, simply staring at Wojtek's smiling face turned lovingly towards his guardian, who looks equally smitten. I can almost feel the warmth of his furry body, hear his gentle growls and the joyful shouts of the soldiers as Wojtek wrestles with one of them, probably Irek.

Overwhelmingly emotional feelings wash over me; so much so that I make a momentous decision. Here and now I, Emil Bartowski, promise you Wojtek, my brother and my comrades, that your story, our story, will be told.

* * *

CHAPTER 2

From a frozen wasteland to the heat of the Middle East and Wojtek's Country

In July, 1941 after the Germans had invaded Russia, the Polish Government In Exile in London signed the Polish-Soviet Agreement, which led to a resumption of diplomatic relations and enabled the release of all Polish detainees from brutal Soviet labour camps. My family were amongst them; my parents Jozef and Bronislawa, my three brothers Bolek, Wladziu and Kaziu; two sisters, Jozia and Jasia and myself. I was the oldest. We and so many like us, had been cruelly ripped without warning from our homes by the Russian army, forced to literally leave at a moment's notice, grabbing what possessions we could.

We had originally been taken by the Soviets to these camps in the isolated wilderness of Siberia, scene of such unimaginable human suffering, including starvation, frostbite and disease. The incredibly severe winters were the most difficult to endure; there were times when the temperature dropped to -60 0C. You could never imagine such intense cold and the feeling of being so hungry that you would be grateful for a scrap of bread, no matter how old. I cannot understand the modern Western preoccupation with diets. People who experienced similar hardships regard such vain self obsession as an insult; even a sin. To have food and either severely restrict how much you eat (unless there is a medical reason) or throw it away would even now be seen as an unimaginable crime by those who knew what real hunger meant.

Bodies contaminated by typhoid dropped like flies. The fact that all of my family managed to later get out of there alive was in itself a miracle.

After our release from this tortuous prison, we and thousands of others like us had to go to Uzbekhistan, where Generals Sikorski and Anders were forming a Polish army, which would in effect be under British command. Anders would be leading this newly established army.

Not all the newly freed Poles then had the same destinations. Families whose kin had joined the newly formed Polish army and who would fight alongside the Allies in the battles of Normandy and Monte Cassino (including my own, as Bolek and I had enlisted in such a Company) travelled to Persia (now Iran) and Pakistan escorted by British forces. After that, as a result of a deal between Winston Churchill and the two Polish generals, they were shipped to South Africa with a British army contingent who were to be stationed in Rhodesia. They were then taken to Arusha in Tanzania, where a camp was set up overseen by a British Captain. They were to have their own memorable experiences and adventures there for a few years before being brought by passenger ship to England after the war.

One of my younger brothers Wladziu, joined the Polish Cadets (Junacka Szkola Mechaniczna), as at the age of fourteen, he was too young to actually enlist, though he would be spending time in Egypt and Palestine. Thankfully, he wouldn't be seeing any action, but instead learn technical skills.

Poland has always taken education very seriously and its people had either completed their education if they were old enough to join the army, or were taught whilst in the cadets or army. It happened that due to their circumstances, some of the soldier's education might have been interrupted, but they had at least learnt basic literacy and numeracy skills. There was never any question of anyone not going to school. The ones that stayed in England after the war generally completed some form of education or practical training here, in spite of the fact that they first had to overcome the language barrier. However, Poles are resilient, persistent and willing to learn.

My brother Bolek and I were the oldest at twenty and twenty one respectively and as such, were keen to enrol in General Anders' newly formed army contingent which had been part of the Agreement. We joined the 22nd Company Polish Army Service Corps 3522 (Artillery).

Our route would take us via Persia to Egypt, Palestine, then Italy. We all prayed that one day soon our scattered family would safely be reunited. In fact, it wouldn't be until 1948 that we would all see each other again. During that time, everyone found a spiritual strength they didn't know they possessed. Faith and trust in God sustained us, as it has always done.

It was in April 1942, that our unit and others landed in Persia on the edges of the Caspian Sea. We had landed in the port of Pahlevi and were making our way in army trucks through the mountainous terrain en route from the ancient town of Hamadan to Kangavar, when we encountered a new soldier who was to become part of our Company and our lives forever.

* * *

CHAPTER 3

Meeting Wojtek

Although it was not quite yet summer, the heat from the midday sun was intense, as we wound our way through the mountains in a small convoy of trucks. I was in the first open vehicle with Bolek and a few others, enjoying the breeze blowing through my hair, whilst the sun beat down on us as we made our way along the rough, bumpy, mountain track, which was lined with trees on one side, whilst on the other there was a thick shady forest, which seemed to stretch for miles.

We had been driving for hours. I was sitting behind my brother and as I sleepily looked at Bolek's short, thick, wavy, fair hair in front of me, I was glad that at least being in the same Company I could keep an eye on him. I had promised my parents I would. I was still staring at his flaxen crop, thinking how weird it felt for my siblings and I that Bolek was so fair and pale, as we were all able to tan easily and had black hair, though I suppose it wasn't so strange really, as our father had been blonde in his youth. All of us, including my parents, were lucky to have what we used to call our 'trademark' piercing light blue eyes. Our neighbours back in Poland would often comment on them.

The hard wooden seats felt even more uncomfortable after the jerky ride and we were all in need of refreshments and the opportunity to stretch our legs. Henio our driver suddenly braked to a screeching halt. We were thrown forwards. Stas, who was rather podgy and quite breathless in the midday heat, actually came off his seat and landed on the dusty floor of the truck with a painful bump.

'Hey! What are you doing? I nearly fell off the truck!'

'Watch it Henio!' some of us called out in protest. Henio just laughed. He had a bit of a wild sense of fun and was always telling jokes. 'I thought this would be a good place to wake you up and stop for a tea break guys!' He opened his door and jumped out.

'You're mad!' shouted Stas, trying to get up and regain some of his dignity. He didn't appreciate the joke.

'What's the problem Stas? You've enough padding for a soft landing!' joked Henio cheekily in reply.

The trucks behind ours also stopped. Pawel, the driver immediately behind us looked flustered. He bellowed at Henio, 'You crazy man! I could have gone into the back of you. Don't do that again!'

Our Lance Corporal Peter Prendys emerged from the other side of the truck. He gave Henio a stern schoolteacher like glance, as if he was telling off a naughty pupil. Respect for him and indeed the other officers was so strong that nothing needed to be said. The look spoke volumes. 'Sorry sir,' apologised Henio, slightly abashed.

Lance Corporal Prendys called to Irek, another of our 'gang', who was also the strongest. 'Irek, get the boxes of rations will you? Just the tea, bread and corned beef.'

Irek liked to work out with whatever objects he could wherever we were camped and looked like a body builder. Add to that the fact that he was probably the tallest of any of our Company and you can imagine the looks of admiration drawn by this 'superhero-looking' specimen of a man wherever our travels took us.

We all got off our trucks and strolled over to the side of the road. Several of us decided to relax under the cool shade of the trees. Some lit cigarettes. Nearly everyone smoked in those days. We were just sitting down to enjoy our much anticipated provisions, when a loud rustling could be heard behind us. We froze. Remember, this was wartime. Every man reached for his revolver and worriedly looked around, eyes darting from tree to tree, occasionally blinded by brilliant flickers of sunshine in between the tall trunks and luscious leaves. No one spoke, until Captain Kipiniak who had been in the truck behind, called out loudly, 'Who's there? Show yourself, now!'

A bit more rustling and the sound of twigs breaking under foot cut through the silence, then a small figure emerged. It was a young Persian boy who was about twelve years old I'd guess, with a swarthy complexion, large, saucer like dark eyes, framed by a thin, drawn face. He was attired in the local fashion, albeit slightly grimy. He looked frightened, like a young deer that had been stopped in its tracks by its predator.

He was holding some sort of bundle. The boy looked scared and tentatively made his way towards us, eyes staring widely in fear at each of us in turn. Noticing our guns, he panicked, dropped the bundle and put his skinny brown arms up in defence shouting in broken English, 'No shoot! No Shoot!' The Captain cried, 'It's OK! It's OK!' Then more calmly and quietly, he tried to gesture to the boy that he was in no danger. The youth seemed to understand, though he still looked a bit wary. He looked down at the bundle he had placed next to him, which was in fact a worn, rather grubby, Hessian sack. The sack seemed to move slightly, so unnoticeably in fact, that only my brother and I appeared aware that it had done so.

Bolek nudged me and whispered, 'Emil, did you see what I saw?'

'You mean the sack moving?'

We kept a watchful eye on the intriguing object, as Captain Kipiniak tried to communicate with the lad.

'This'll be good,' laughed Henio, his humour revived. 'The boy doesn't speak Polish and not much English by the looks of it and we don't speak Arabic.'

But the captain was undeterred. He continued slowly using sign language and gestures and all at once the boy beamed, revealing an admirable set of dazzling white teeth. 'Yes, yes!' he exclaimed excitedly, put his hand to his mouth, then thrust it in Stas's direction. Stas looked blankly at the captain, holding his half eaten sandwich. 'What?' he asked, appearing not to comprehend. Our Lance Corporal Peter, who had been watching intently, guessed what the boy wanted. 'Stas, the boy's hungry; just look at him, skin and bones. I think he wants your snack.'

'Why mine? You've all got your rations as well.'

The look of horror on Stas's face and his indignant tone made us all burst out laughing. The boy looked at us rather uncertainly, not understanding the cause of our mirth. I'm sure he thought we were laughing at him. Then all of a sudden the sack swayed backwards and forwards quite violently and emitted what could only be described as a loud half yawn, half grunt.

We stopped laughing and focussed our attention on the moving object. The boy started jabbering something in his own language, then bent over and took hold of the top of the sack, starting to pull at the drawstring fastening. Before anyone could do anything, an animal's snout pushed it's way in between the boy's hands and to our utter astonishment, a little brown bear cub's furry head surfaced. Its eyes blinked a few times in the bright daylight, as the boy helped him clamber out of the sack. It emerged in a rather dishevelled state and painfully thin. It too obviously hadn't eaten in a good while. It just sat there staring at us, as if waiting for us to make the next move.

Our faces must have looked a picture. This time we really fell about laughing. Irek stared, 'Well I never.....'

Henio said what we were all thinking. 'Of all the things to find out here, I never expected THIS!'

The bear looked around and it then did something I will never forget. He got up and on all fours ambled across to Lance Corporal Peter Prendys, planted himself in front of him and started making strange noises. Then still fixing his gaze on our officer, he tried to sit up on his hind legs and waved his front paws. When he opened his mouth, he honestly looked like he was smiling. Peter looked down at the amiable creature, stroked its head and said, 'Look, I think he's as hungry as the boy. We'll have to feed them both.' The cub nuzzled his head against Peter's leg.

Stas tried to put his hand holding his sandwich inconspicuously behind his back, but Henio was standing close to him and quick as lightning grabbed the sandwich from Stas's grasp. He threw it towards the cub, who didn't hesitate to dash forwards and pick it up, stuffing it all in his mouth at once. 'Hey, Stas, it even eats like you!' teased Henio. Stas's face turned bright red. The cub licked its lips, went back to The Lance Corporal and sat at his feet, gazing up at the officer. Bolek commented that in the heat of the day, the bear was most likely very thirsty. 'So what do you give a bear to drink?'

'And what from?' soldiers from the other trucks had joined us.

I had an idea. 'Well, as it's a baby, why not give it some of our milk?'

'You're right Emil,' said Lance Corporal Peter. 'Let me think what we can use as a teat, because remember it would normally still be feeding off its mother.' He paused in thought for a moment, then climbed onto the back of the truck and jumped back down triumphantly holding something in his hand. It was the old empty vodka bottle that had been rolling around the back of our vehicle for ages. No-one had bothered to throw it away. Just as well. Peter poured some tinned sweet condensed milk into the bottle, then wrapped an old towel that had been in the front of the truck around the mouth of the bottle, to make a sort of a teat for the cub. After that, he placed the cub on his lap and carefully put the 'teat' to his mouth, tilting it slightly so that the creamy liquid could easily be swallowed by the 'baby'. I wish I'd had my camera with me.

'Hey, Sir! Someone called out. 'It thinks your it's mother!' We observed that Peter looked quite pleased at this remark. Henio couldn't resist. 'Are you going to sing it a lullaby sir?'

Peter just turned to Henio and remarked, 'When was the last time you did a week's kitchen duty Private Dabrowicz?'

Henio took the hint, knowing that he had already pushed the boundaries earlier. 'Sorry sir.'

Years later when reflecting on that first 'weaning' of Wojtek's, my friends and I were convinced that there must have been some drops of vodka left in the bottle, that they had mixed with the milk and that was what first started Wojtek's taste for alcohol.

Whilst the boy hungrily demolished some bread and honey so fast we were afraid he would choke, the Captain and Lance Corporal were trying to understand what the boy was doing with the bear. Don't ask me how, but using more sign language, they managed to find out that the cub's mother had been shot by hunters, meaning that the bear was then wandering around alone, scrounging for food.

The boy had found him and decided to either trade him for food when the occasion arose, as it had today, or if that didn't succeed, to sell him to a circus as a dancing bear, a cruel but accepted custom in that part of the world. Fortunately for the bear (and us) they had come across our convoy at just the right time.

Whilst our two officers were finding out all this information, the bear wouldn't move from Peter's side as it hungrily devoured one sandwich after another that the men had generously offered. The rest of us relaxed on the grass at the side of the road, looking at the scene with interest, whilst munching on our own provisions. 'Do you think it's a girl or boy bear?' wondered Irek.

'How can you tell?' asked Tadek, another of our 'truck gang'.

Henio grinned. 'Well, if it was a girl bear cub it wouldn't stop talking; this one's fairly quiet!'

We all laughed. Jacek, who had been studying Science at university before the outbreak of war and wearing glasses looked quite studious and so had been dubbed 'the professor', stood up. He peered at the cub from one side then another, stating, 'It's definitely a boy.'

We all cheered, don't ask me why. At that point it wouldn't really have mattered what sex the cub was. We finished our food, then stood up and walked over to our trucks. The two officers also stood up and we watched Lance Corporal Prendys go over to the truck and take out a few more tins, including a large tin of corned beef, a bar of chocolate and a Swiss Army knife. Captain Kipiniak took out what looked like coins and some notes from one of his khaki shorts pockets. They stood in front of the boy and all of them shook hands, smiling. Then the boy stuffed the money and other items into the Hessian sack, waved and shouted something, probably 'Bye!' turned and walked back into the wood, disappearing in seconds.

The cub didn't seem at all perturbed by the boy's absence, but instead kept close to Lance Corporal Peter, who was now crouching over him, speaking soothingly, whilst fondling his little ears. Catain Kipiniak asked us all to gather round. He cleared his throat and looking directly at us declared that Wojtek would now officially be our adopted 22nd. Company, Polish Army Service Corps (Artillery) mascot and would be travelling with us wherever we went. He hoped we would all help to look after it. The Persian boy had apparently agreed to 'sell' him to us in return for the money and goods that the two officers had given him. It seems that the corned beef had swung the deal. Everyone cheered again.

We were all thrilled. Our very own pet to love and look after in the middle of the war! Space was readily made for our new addition at the back of the truck, but the Lance Corporal had other ideas. He gently picked up the cub and opening the passenger door to where he had been riding alone just an hour or so ago, announced that the cub would be sitting on his lap at the front, to get a good view of the road. We smiled.

Peter had fallen in love with the bear and the feeling seemed mutual, as the bear appeared to have chosen the officer as its surrogate mother. This of course also meant that he would be its handler, as the bear would grow into a huge animal and though by then no longer be wild, would naturally still need a firm hand. Peter was tall, well built and strong; other attributes necessary for handling the adult Wojtek.

Peter was liked by the men and as one of the oldest officers in the Company, in addition to the fact that his calm, wise, quiet manner was so well respected anyway, was the most evident choice of guardian for our cub.

'He needs a name, ' said Henio, before getting into his seat and starting the engine.

'What about Misiu (little bear)?'

'Eh? He needs a proper name', commented Tadek.

Out of the blue, Bolek suggested, 'What about Wojtek?'

There was a pause as everyone thought about this name for a second, then realised the significance of it. 'Perfect!' we all cried out as one.

Henio explained aloud what we had all been thinking. 'Yes, it's ideal for him, because in Polish Wojciech (the formal form of Wojtek) means 'Happy Warrior'; the cub had a smile on his face and he'll now be a sort of a warrior by becoming a soldier like us in our army.'

The truck began to move off slowly with its extra unanticipated passenger on board. Peter held the cub tenderly in his arms and said softly, 'Hello Wojtek. Welcome to our Company, your new home. You're one of us now my little friend.'

* * *

Lance Corporal Peter Prendys And Wojtek
'Smile for the camera Wojtek!'

CHAPTER 4

Raising Wojtek

As our convoy continued its journey through the picturesque mountain terrain en route to our first army base, the sun gradually hid its cheery smile behind gloomy, grey clouds. A cool breeze pervaded the air and our spirits somehow changed to match nature's mood. Earlier spontaneous euphoria was replaced by a calmer, more rational frame of mind, as we began to wonder about the consequences of what we had done. Not that we regretted it – not at all, there was no doubt about having done the right thing in taking Wojtek with us.

It was just that we had bought Wojtek without really thinking it through properly. Our main concern was the Commanding Officer's reaction to meeting the very young bear cub. Would Major Chelkowski allow us to keep this loveable creature? What if he didn't? The thought of that dampened our elation somewhat at first, until that is, our faith came to the fore and we all felt the conviction that Wojtek was meant to be ours. There was no need to worry.

We were to be proved correct. We eventually arrived at our first army base in Palestine. Just as a precaution until we had gauged the C.O's mood and had decided on the most appropriate time for the two to meet, we kept Wojtek well away from the officer's accommodation. Don't ask me how we managed it, as the cub had the mischievous curiosity of an inquisitive child, eager to discover the world around him and so would try to run to part of the camp boundaries, one or two soldiers in hot pursuit.

Eventually, the day came when Major Chelkowski and Wojtek were introduced to each other. One sweet, innocent look was all it too to charm the Major. The tall officer bent over to stroke Wojtek, who was sitting quietly in front of him, chewing a bread and honey (what else?) sandwich. He was on his best behaviour, as if realising the importance of making a good first impression. Wojtek suddenly gave Chelkowski his now trademark grin.

The major stroked his black moustache thoughtfully, then stood up, straightened his back and said, 'Lance Corporal Prendys; I hereby make you official warden and handler of our new and very welcome mascot. You and Wojtek will have your own quarters. We will arrange that in the next couple of days. Until then, I think it will be for the best if Wojtek sleeps in MY tent.' Peter stared in disbelief first at the C.O, then at Wojtek, unsure as to what had surprised him the most; the Major allowing him to have his very own quarters with Wojtek, a most exceptional concession; or the fact that he actually wanted Wojtek to stay with him in his officer's tent for a while! Slightly dazed, but extremely happy, Peter led Wojtek back to our tents. When he told us the good news, we shared his incredulity and joy. Wojtek was officially ours!

Actually, it had been a wise move on behalf of the amiable but shrewd officer, who realised that this bear would not only be a perfect mascot for his men, but more importantly, a great morale booster during the trials of this war; something for these soldiers so far away from their families to love and help them to cope with the stressful situation they were in.

Peter and Wojtek moved into their own accommodation. What an honour! We soldiers slipped in and out of the pair's new canvas 'home' to play with our cub whenever our duties would allow.

Wojtek was just like a little child. For certain (short) periods of time when Peter and the rest of us were busy about our duties, just like a toddler kept in its playpen, he was kept on a fairly long restraining tether which was tied to a post. Whenever he was released from it, he would delight in running in and out of the tent and round it, for someone to chase him, pick him up and cuddle him, then take him back to either tie him up again or hand him back to Peter. Either that, or he would enjoy a playful tussle with someone who wouldn't mind rolling around the ground and be sat on by him.

The Lance Corporal's maternal instinct earned him the affectionate nickname of Mother Bear. He gave Wojtek his milk and cuddled him when he seemed tired, or something had scared him. The cub would even creep into Peter's bed at night for a warm, comforting cuddle. In the cold evenings, you could see Wojtek's sweet little face just peeking out of Peter's protective, warm greatcoat, where the wee cub would snuggle secure and warm.

So far as Wojtek was concerned, he was with his family.

* * *

CHAPTER 5

Wojtek gets stuck in a tree & other adventures

One morning, Peter woke to find that Wojtek wasn't in his bed – yes, he really had a bed- and just as he was sleepily considering getting up to see where his young charge was, he suddenly heard loud whimpering. Wojtek!

Peter, still half dressed ran outside, anxiously looking around to see from which direction the painful sounds were emanating. He reached the tall, elegant palm trees on the other side of the camp and stood motionless for a moment in focussed concentration. The whimpering became more urgent and Peter, standing near a huge palm tree, worriedly looked all around him. Where *was* Wojtek?

By this time, the rest of us near Peter's quarters had heard the commotion and had joined our comrade outside. 'Where is he sir?' asked Tadek, my old friend from school who had joined the same Company, straining his eyes as he peered into the distance for any sign of the little cub. Peter's unease made him snap. 'If I knew that, I'd have found him by now!' he replied uncharacteristically sharply.

'Sorry sir, I'm worried about him as well you know,' said Tadek quietly. He had a good heart, as well as being good with practical tasks and always volunteered to help out if Peter was called for extra duties. The Lance Corporal also apologised and smiled at his comrade. 'Thanks for coming to help.' The pathetic whining had sounded very close, though it had temporarily abated.

As our eyes scanned the immediate area around us, the wide, green, fan-like leaves of the mature palm tree next to us started to shake and some of them floated gently to the ground, landing near to our feet. We looked up just as there was a loud grunt and there, holding onto a sturdy branch for dear life, sharp claws on his feet trying to grip another less stable branch below, was our Wojtek.

He was staring down at us in desperation and his face was a picture. He looked both terrified and annoyed at the same time. We all started laughing, as a very relieved Peter stared up at his young charge saying incredulously. 'What the …..what on earth are you doing up there, you bundle of mischief?'

Wojtek calmed down somewhat at seeing his 'Mother Bear' below, but then all his pent up anxiety seemed to spill out as he emitted a stream of distressed noises, as if complaining about his predicament. Cue more raucous laughter. Peter turned to Bolek. 'Go and fetch the ladder for me would you Private? I don't think he's going to manage to get down on his own. I'll have to climb up and get him.'

A few minutes later Bolek returned with the requested item and carefully leaned it against the tree. Peter took off his beret and tucked it under the strap on his shoulder. 'Hold it steady for me would you lads? I'm going up.'

My brother and I clutched the sides of the ladder firmly as Peter climbed to the top. Tadek waited close by, ready to help if needed. Wojtek became very quiet and waited confidently for his 'mother' to fetch him. He knew he was safe now. A few minutes later, Peter carefully descended with our little friend and when the Lance Corporal reached the bottom rung of the ladder, we applauded enthusiastically amid calls of 'Well done sir!'

On reaching terra firma, Wojtek still clutched Peter's hand tightly and when the soldier knelt down next to him speaking in calm, reassuring tones, he was rewarded with a loving, very grateful kiss from his 'child'.

Wojtek learnt his lessons quickly. He still climbed up palm trees, but he had realised that if he was going to get to the top on his own, he would also have to work out his own way to descend safely.

The rest of us soldiers meanwhile, had also been taught something significant. We were beginning to realise that just as you need eyes in the back of your head for very young children, so you need them for junior bear cubs!

For most of our time so close to the hot Palestine desert, we didn't feel as if we were at war. We were in effect marking time, awaiting orders from General Anders and we were kept occupied by training exercises and manoeuvres. And of course there was Wojtek, who gave us such joy!

It seems funny writing about happiness during wartime and us about to be in the thick of it. Looking after and playing with our loveable friend made us feel at times as if there was no war.

Our duties included ferrying supplies to other posts in the Middle East and frequently when we embarked on such a journey, Wojtek would accompany us, sitting in the front passenger seat of Peter's cab, happily taking in the view around him. He was a born traveller and seemed to enjoy the gasps of astonished disbelief from passers by or villagers whenever they spotted the bear riding with us. Wojtek loved being the centre of attention.

As he grew into an adolescent bear, his physical size

obviously also increased until his height reached over 6' and he weighed over 500 lbs.

This meant amongst other things, that fun wrestling bouts became a bit more physical, although Wojtek was always gentle with us and would never intentionally hurt anyone.

Once, bets were made amongst the camp soldiers as to who would win such a bout between our bear and Irek, the 'muscle monster'. 'Win' just meant that either Irek would be pinned to the ground (gently) by our other gentle giant, or that Irek would manage to sit on him for five seconds. There was a lot of good natured shouting and whistling during the 'match'. Needless to say, the bear won. 'Irek, you fight like a girl!' shouted Henio, clapping Wojtek on the back. 'Oh yeh? Come here and say that and we'll see who's the girl!' Henio ran towards the kitchen tent, where he took some fruit and honey and gave it to the victorious Wojtek.

I'd just like to mention here that Wojtek was *never* forced to participate in these games. He himself used to initiate play wrestling from an early age and other human behaviours he exhibited more and more as he became older were not cruelly imposed upon him either by any of us. We loved Wojtek. We couldn't ever hurt him. Besides, he had a strong will and mind of his own and wouldn't do anything he didn't want to!

After watching the friendly wrestling bout, Henio himself sat down on the ground next to Wojtek, looking forward to quenching his thirst with a bottle of beer. Just as he was about to take a swig from it, Henio saw that Wojtek hadn't touched his provisions, but was staring intently at the beer bottle. Henio thought for a moment and then said with a twinkle in his eye, 'Would you like to try some, our big furry friend?' Peter, standing nearby didn't look too sure, but hesitatingly gave his permission. 'Well, just give him a bit then. I don't know what effect alcohol will have on him.'

So Henio drank the best part of the contents, whilst Wojtek patiently waited in anticipation, as if he knew that his turn would come. He managed to hold the bottle in his large paws (he had great dexterity) and tipped the warm contents down his throat, just like he'd observed Henio do. The latter looked on speechless, then let out a low whistle. 'Did you see that?' he breathed. As he turned round to us laughingly, there was a loud smash that made him and us jump. Wojtek's method of discarding empty beer bottles would be to simply throw them in any direction after he'd imbued the liquid! Someone would usually have to remember to call out the warning 'Duck!' after he'd finished his quota, as from then on, Wojtek would enjoy innumerable bottles of his favourite tipple as a reward for good behaviour.

He also made friends with a neighbouring British regiment's Dalmatian dog. Our bear loved games of 'chase' and once when he was being pursued playfully by some of the soldiers, he rushed around the tents and glancing behind him to see where they were instead of where he was going, he tripped over and fell headlong over a tent guy rope, right on top of the sleeping Dalmatian.

The dog was not amused. He leapt to his feet and stared at Wojtek, growling deeply. Wojtek remained seated on the ground, quite still. For a few seconds, they seemed to be sizing each other up. Suddenly, the dog began to wag his tail and rubbed himself against the surprised bear, licking his face. Wojtek, on feeling such friendliness, to everyone's delight, decided to reciprocate. Their friendship was sealed.

Their favourite game of course was 'chase' and it usually involved the dog running very fast, with Wojtek close behind, then his canine friend would unexpectedly brake hard mid-pursuit, whilst Wojtek ran into him, then rolled over and over in the dust. They never seemed to tire of the same game that gave them and the soldiers from both camps a great deal of enjoyment.

Nevertheless, Wojtek reacted differently to certain other types of animals, such as horses, donkeys and cows. I remember there was one incident when near to our campsite, which was bordered from one side by a village and some fields, Wojtek took it upon himself to explore. We still don't know how his tether came loose, though fortunately Peter had to go to his tent for something and saw the restraint left trailing on the floor and went off to find Wojtek.

Our bear had wandered towards one of the fields and spotted a horse in the distance. Now I need to explain that Wojtek usually ambled around the camp on his hind legs, walking like a man. He would now demonstrate on more than one instance, that when confronting other animals such as the one he was about to encounter, the natural predator in him would sometimes emerge and he would drop to all fours, moving slowly and purposefully towards his intended prey. This was such an occasion.

The huge, old, black mare had been nonchalantly grazing in the field, when she must have sensed danger. She looked around and spotted Wojtek slowly and menacingly making his way through the field. As the bear speeded up towards the horse and stood on his hind legs growling at him loudly, the terrified horse all at once reared up onto its hind legs also and kicked Wojtek on his head. It then ran off in the opposite direction. Wojtek shocked and stunned, turned round and dizzily began to stumble back towards the camp, which is when Peter caught up with him, ready to read him the riot act before giving him a great hug. Fortunately it was just Wojtek's pride that had really been hurt, but that was the last time he approached a horse. Another lesson learnt!

I recall one unpleasant occasion when we felt very afraid for our friend. A Polish Infantry outfit, the 16th. Lwow Rifles Battalion, also happened to have a bear as their mascot, called Michael, in memory of Michael Karaszewicz-Tokarzewski, the Polish general who had been given the bear cub as a gift from the Shah Of Persia. This great hulk was older than Wojtek and of a very aggressive disposition, though we weren't aware of that when a meeting between the two giants was initially agreed and arranged. On meeting Wojtek, Michael went crazy. He pulled and wrenched at his leash, until, despite the best efforts of his keepers, broke free and made for our bear.

Wojtek seemed to have sensed danger the moment he laid eyes on the antagonistic 'guest'. At first he just observed Michael in silence. In fact he wouldn't take his eyes off him. When that monster lunged for Wojtek, the latter stood up looking straight at him, then roaring loudly lifted his large front paws in defence, claws at the ready. We'd never seen him like this. We were partly in awe of him, but also afraid for him. Michael was even bigger than Wojtek.

The two fought fiercely for what seemed like ages and

the terrifying sounds they made during their battle made us feel sick. They both snarled and roared constantly, every so often their large, powerful fangs trying to dig into each other's necks. They lunged at each other with massive, heavy paws. The bears were attacking each other so savagely, that all we could do was watch and pray that Wojtek would come out without being hurt too badly. I put my arm on Peter's shoulder for the whole time. He was shaking and couldn't watch.

Finally, they were still locked together in combat until somehow Wojtek used all his force to free himself from the clinch and with what energy he could still summon, pushed the bully Michael away towards his owners. They acted quickly, grabbing hold of him with all their strength, before tethering him and pulling him away. Wojtek had emerged victorious! His first (and fortunately last) major fight and he had won, a true soldier.

We all ran towards our brother as one and were relieved to see that he only had minor injuries. Some of us actually wiped away emotional tears. You can imagine the attention and treats piled on him that night. Peter quietly stuck close by his side for the rest of the evening.

Another creature who was not exactly friendly – in fact a nuisance for Wojtek as well as ourselves, was an initially quite evil little monkey named Kaska. I can't actually recall how she came to be part of our Company, or even why she was allowed to stay with us for as long as she did, considering the nasty little tricks she used to get up to. Probably because she was very pleasant to the Sergeant – Major who looked after her as her guardian and a few chosen others.

Kaska had the unpleasant habit of pilfering our food

and possessions, or creating some kind of chaos, such as throwing clothes and cigarettes around our tents, or hiding other personal items.

Wojtek dreaded her presence, as it usually involved some kind of unpleasantness for himself as a target for her tricks, in addition to the fact that she liked to steal some of his limelight. As soon as she appeared, Wojtek would run a mile.

The monkey could be amusing on occasions, such as when she dressed in the skirt and blouse of a Polish female soldier and decided to run after someone, hitching up her skirt as she did so, her skinny, hairy brown legs racing around the camp.

However, most of us tired of her devious tricks and longed for something to be done to stop them. Eventually, after the battle at Monte Cassino, someone had the bright idea of introducing her to a male of the species in order to get her pregnant with the aim of calming her down; that having a young one to look after might distract her from causing trouble. Thus she was taken to the zoo in Rome by the Sergeant-Major to achieve this objective.

She did indeed get impregnated whilst spending some time there and the result was a baby boy. The newborn had the required effect on Kaska. She stopped the vicious, troublesome behaviour and even seemed to make an effort to be friendlier towards Wojtek. The rest of us became quite fond of her.

Unfortunately, a short time later, the baby died of tuberculosis. Kaska was heartbroken and it pained us all to see her obvious distress. Her spirit was crushed and nothing seemed to interest her. Wojtek sensed her grief and eventually dared to approach the monkey. When he didn't get a negative reaction, he stayed with her for periods of time, licking her, as if trying to console his one time enemy. Wojtek demonstrated forgiveness, kindness and compassion more than any human I have ever known. When Kaska died of a broken heart, Wojtek mourned her as an old friend.

* * *

CHAPTER 6

Water baby Wojtek & the spy

Wojtek with his thick fur coat, found it difficult to cope with the intense heat during the summers, particularly considering that he had been used to the more temperate climate in the mountains. Thus it was decided that he needed a helping hand to keep cool.

We would dig a hole, fill it with water and Wojtek would lie in it for hours, trying to keep as chilled as possible. In fact, he loved water and would literally follow the men whenever they went to the shower unit, hoping to be deluged with it. Obviously this wasn't possible on a frequent basis, as we were very close to a desert, so you can imagine how careful we had to be with our water supply. However, we knew how much Wojtek needed to keep cool and this was another method when possible.

Wojtek simply loved having showers. After watching us go in and turn them on, he had very cleverly learnt to copy our methods. Our first reaction had been one of amazement, but not for long, as we had realised that there was something very special about this bear. As a result of his newly acquired skill, we had to try to keep the showers locked when not in use.

It so happened that in these showers Wojtek would unexpectedly become a hero. During one particularly baking hot afternoon, it was very quiet around the base and Wojtek decided he would try his luck with a quick sprinkle. Maybe someone was using the facilities in the ablutions hut and he could sneak in for a quick, refreshing wash.

Wojtek strolled up to the door and to his great delight, saw that it was open. Brilliant! He heard a noise, like feet shuffling, but no sound of water spraying or dripping. Wondering which of his soldier friends were inside, he sauntered in, only to see the back of a complete stranger, a male dressed in a traditional white Arabic robe; a stiff red fez sitting on his dark head. The man had clearly just got into the hut, oblivious of the huge animal that had followed him inside. He heard heavy breathing and a sort of low growl and swung round to see Wojtek raised on his hind legs and baring his teeth.

There was a terrible banshee-like scream that alerted the whole base. Me, Peter, Irek, Tadek and Bolek were the closest and reached the hut in a flash, whilst the guards ran across to see what the problem was.

As we dashed into the hut, the scene was one that I shall never forget.

There shaking in the corner, was the petrified Arab, absolute terror etched on his swarthy, sweaty, bearded face; his eyes bulging with fear and fixed on Wojtek. He was babbling something in his native tongue and when he saw us come inside, fell on his knees, hands clutched tightly together as in prayer, begging for help and mercy. Wojtek was just standing there, still on his hind legs, clutching the stranger's red fez in his paws so tightly that it completely squashed; the black toggle on top of it swaying madly. Wojtek let out a triumphant roar. After the initial shock, we all cheered. Our clever, brave, loyal bear had caught a spy!

As the guards led the quivering intruder away for

interrogation, which is when he admitted to being a spy, the Arab was still crying uncontrollably. It transpired later under questioning, that he had managed to break through the base perimeter and creep into the shower hut, which had been left open.

His plan was apparently to wait until nightfall, when he would attempt to locate the camp's weapons arsenal. However, the thought had never crossed his mind that there might be a bear lurking on the premises!

Wojtek was the toast of the base and hailed a hero. As a much deserved reward, he was given his favourite snacks as treats, in addition to beer and a very long shower!

Yes, Wojtek was quite a water baby. He really enjoyed swimming and got very excited when allowed to join the men for a dip in a river or lake.

He had a habit of diving under water for a few seconds, then popping up unexpectedly next to someone. We had a lot of fun at the local's expense, when they went swimming unawares and Wojtek would surface out of the blue, sometimes with a shocked, wriggling fish between his jaws, causing many shrieking scenes of panic. We would always dash over straightaway and guide Wojtek back to our end of his 'pool', explaining to the stunned, frightened villagers that Wojtek was actually quite tame and was just playing a game, with no intention of hurting anyone. Needless to say, on several occasions we were asked not to return.

※ ※ ※

CHAPTER 7

Wojtek has an eye for the girls

I recall with great amusement one occasion when Wojtek showed what an absolute charmer with ladies he could be.

Our Company was delivering supplies to a large Allied forces military camp in Iraq. It so happened that women soldiers were also part of this camp. Whilst we soldiers were busy either unloading the supplies and handing them to the others from the base, or having a cigarette with them, Wojtek wandered off to explore.

He had prowled around for a little while and was starting to feel a little bored. There didn't seem to be any tasty snacks around and he was getting hungry. Maybe Peter would get him something to eat. He was just about to turn back, when a strange sight caught his eye and made him stop in his tracks.

There floating in the warm breeze suspended from a string, was a line of washing; freshly washed women's underwear to be precise (and as it transpired later, newly bought). Wojtek was fascinated. He walked up to the line on his hind legs and pulled everything off, one of the bras dropping onto his head. The gentle giant sauntered off happily with his find, large paws clutching the pile of smalls, the bra carelessly dangling around his ears.

Meanwhile, one of the female soldiers had just come round from the back of her tent to collect her washing, when she was met with this unbelievable sight. She was too terrified to scream; she couldn't make any audible sound except for a tiny squeak and her legs refused to move.

She backed towards the tent entrance, not daring to turn her back on the enormous brown bear, not having heard of Wojtek and so thinking he was dangerous. When she got inside the tent, the female Private described what she had just witnessed to her friends in a stage whisper. Astonished and scared, they cautiously tiptoed over to the flap, pulled it back and nervously poked their heads out.

Seeing the bear carrying their 'essentials' into the distance, they yelled so loud you could have heard them in the next town. Peter, me, Bolek and Jacek on hearing the high pitched screams, of one mind dashed over in their direction. On the way we met Wojtek, who had decided to stop for a rest and examine his wares. He was quite calmly shredding the lingerie with his sharp claws, the bra still sitting on his head, oblivious to the panic he had caused.

We laughed so much the tears flowed and our sides hurt. Peter composed himself first and he somehow managed to keep a straight face as he wagged his finger in front of Wojtek's snout, whilst taking the offending items of him, one at a time. 'What have I told you about taking things that don't belong to you?' he said sternly, trying to sound annoyed. Wojtek just sat there, staring at his guardian, but when all the items had been confiscated, including the one perched on his head, he rolled over onto his back and lay there with his sturdy legs in the air, until Peter relented and gave him a cuddle.

Of course some of us saw this as an ideal opportunity to meet the young women soldiers. We decided to pay them a visit with Wojtek, so that he could apologise. Thus a little while later, after smartening ourselves up a bit, a small group of us went over to explain what had happened and about our playful young charge. At first, the women were wary of going anywhere near Wojtek, but he looked quite sorry for himself and after a little while, some of them even ventured to pat him on the head.

As the atmosphere became more amenable, we couldn't believe what Wojtek did next. He actually flirted with the women! Yes, our bear had 'a way with the ladies' and proved he could charm himself out of trouble.

He covered his eyes with his paws, then peeped out from behind them at the girls, who would squeal in delight. 'Isn't he a handsome bear!'

'So lovely and cuddly.' Cue Wojtek looking appealing, lying on his back again, his mouth smilingly open. 'Aaah, isn't he sweet? I'm going to fetch him some bread and honey.' Wojtek couldn't believe his luck when the sandwich was brought to him and he grabbed it enthusiastically.

He relished the attention and the effect he was having on the women. Us men simply looked on in dumbfounded admiration, while he demolished his welcome snack. We felt a little peeved. We had competition from a bear. The women seemed more interested in Wojtek than they were in us, although it had given us a good excuse to venture over. As it happened, that wouldn't be the last time Wojtek exhibited his new found talent.

* * *

'Room for Wojtek, ladies?'

CHAPTER 8

Empathy & Cigarettes

The most anticipated part of our desert sojourn was probably 'post delivery day' when we would receive letters and cards from our family and friends wherever they were in the world.

At such times, we would retreat to our own quiet corners and read the latest news from our loved ones, look at photographs and generally escape from the war for a little while, daydreaming our way to a spiritual closeness with those we hadn't seen for so long. These letters of course were deliberately upbeat and positive to maintain our morale, though they were also full of aching hearts. You often tried to read between the lines to see if there was any hint of a problem somewhere, but the writers carefully avoided any such oversights. They could only imagine how we felt. They knew we were preparing for battle and the possible likely consequences. Our families were brave as soldiers in their own way, for they refused to mention their worries or problems, so as not to cause us anxiety or frustration.

Bolek and I would get a letter each, but in the same envelope. It was my turn to open the letter this time and we eagerly unfolded the thin squared sheets filled with news from Africa. There was a photo included to show us our family's new home; a round mud hut with a dry straw roof. Our parents and siblings stood in a line in front of it and even though it was a black and white photograph, their dark suntans were obvious and showed evidence of their time in a hot country. They were all there except for Jozia, who was now a sister in the hospital near to their village and had caught malaria poor thing and of course Wladziu was also missing from the group, as he was still in Palestine with the Cadets. It occurred to me that we hadn't heard from him in a good while. Maybe his letter would come next week. Bolek started chuckling as he sat under the welcome shade of a sturdy palm.

I assumed that my youngest brother and sister Kaziu and Jasia had been up to some childish prank. As I went into our tent and looked at my own letter, I was proved correct.

My family had settled in their refugee camp in a village in Tanzania, not far from the jungle and a small lake. Jasia, who was eight and five year old Kaziu had decided to experiment with the long 'Tarzan ropes'; strong vines that hung from the enormous old jungle trees near their mud huts, trying to swing from one tree to another and my little brother had fallen in the water, which fortunately was quite shallow at present, as it hadn't rained for a long time.

Jasia had managed to swing successfully on such a vine from one side of the narrowest part of the lake to the other, jumping onto firm, muddy ground and throwing the vine to Kaziu. He however, somehow misjudged the distance. He jumped up on his little legs, but missed the vine and ended up in the water. Jasia was horrified, not realising that the water was very shallow at that point and started screaming.

When my parents heard her yelling for help, they just dropped everything and panic stricken, dashed off in the direction of the urgent cries. The local waters were known to attract toothy, hungry crocodiles. Almost immediately on arrival at their camp, my family had learnt the old adage; 'When chased by a crocodile, always run in a crooked line'. However, children will be children and will always want to explore areas they have been told not to. The element of risk makes it all the tastier.

So it was that day. The children's usual afternoon rest time had proved a bit boring for them that day and so they had decided to venture out of the immediate camp vicinity for a bit of excitement. The cool, inviting lake had temptingly drawn them to itself and the prospective thrill of attempting the jungle swings had proved too difficult to resist.

They were having a great time laughing, joking and shimmying up the jungle vines until Kaziu fell into the river. Fortunately, he had scrambled out of the water very quickly and though a bit shocked, soaking wet and covered in mud, as he had slipped in his hurry to crawl off the dirty banks, was not in any danger. Jasia instinctively threw her arms round him. Just as my parents arrived on the scene, they saw their two children safe and holding onto each other tightly. Jasia let go of her brother when she saw them and started crying. My Mum gave her a quick kiss on the forehead and said, 'It's alright love, we're here now.' My father's face was expressionless. Kaziu looked sheepish. My parent's first reaction was naturally one of relief and they gave him such a tight hug he couldn't breathe. Then they just as naturally gave Kaziu a scolding he would never forget. Jasia as the oldest and so should have known better, was also reprimanded.

The rest of the letter described the state of my family's health and day to day activities, punctuated by questions about myself and Bolek and love for us both. It might not sound very exciting, but it was exactly what Bolek and I needed. At night in our mind's eye, we would picture the stunning red gold African sunset gracefully setting behind Mount Kilimanjaro, whilst our families settled in their hut for the night, amidst the subdued Masai tribal songs humming quietly in the background.

This was a strange, surreal time in the war. Who could have guessed way back early in September, 1939 when we were all sat round our kitchen table as the Germans marched over the hill on the other side of the fields near to our farmhouse in Przemysl, towards us, that a few years later we would still be in the midst of the war separated by its evil ways and simultaneously experiencing such different lives, albeit temporarily? That was after our country had suffered some of the worst atrocities in its history, first at the hands of the Nazis and then the Russians.

Bolek popped his head round the entrance to our quarters. His blue eyes were sparkling with joy. 'Emil! What did you think of your letter? Kaziu got himself into trouble again eh?' He came in and threw himself on his bed. We were discussing the contents of our mail when we heard a shout from outside. 'Everyone out for a group photo! Photo for your families!' Henio repeated the order and we heard everyone else gathering just near the kitchen tent. We carefully put our letters away safely in our small cardboard boxes that had previously contained tins of corned beef (and still smelled of them) and made our way to join the others.

As we walked up to the makeshift bench to Henio, who had taken on the role of company photographer, I noticed Tadek sitting in front of his tent, staring at a letter in his hand. He looked a million miles away. I turned to

Bolek and said, 'Save me a place next to you, will you? I'm just going to have a word with Tadek.' Bolek glanced over in the direction of our friend and nodded, understandingly.

'O.K Emil. But hurry up, or Henio will take the photo anyway. You know what he's like; great bloke, but the word patience isn't really in his vocabulary!'

As Bolek walked off, I turned round about to go over to Tadek, when I saw the most touching sight of Wojtek, who, it turned out, had just contentedly emerged from the nearby kitchen tent after a hearty meal of fruit and marmalade, seating himself with a hefty thud on the ground next to the soldier.

Intrigued as to what Wojtek was doing, I hung around, keeping my distance. Tadek buried his head in his hands, still clutching his correspondence. A few seconds later, Tadek still had his dark head bent over his knees, Wojtek also still peacefully by his side. He seemed to sense the soldier's distress and wanted to comfort him just by staying as close as he could, like a huge, cuddly teddy bear.

As I stood staring at them, waiting for something to happen I suppose, Wojtek unexpectedly put a huge paw on Tadek's's shoulder. Tadek didn't seem surprised by this action, but just turned and put his arms around the warm, reassuring, furry body. This touching scene actually brought a tear to my eye. Our bear's heart was filled with such love and compassion.

It transpired later that Tadek had received news and photos from his wife Zosia and their three year old son Stefan. He hadn't seen them since Stefan was born and with the uncertainty of the next few months, didn't know when or if he would see them again. Wojtek had approached Tadek just as he was starting to feel overwhelmed with emotion.

Henio was bellowing, 'Come ON, lets get on with it you stragglers! Emil, Jacek, Tadek, Wojtek, get your cheeks on this bench NOW!'

Hesitatingly, I walked up to the pair sitting together, not sure whether to interrupt this private moment. Wojtek looked up at me calmly, somehow kindly. I mouthed 'Thank you' to him and patted his head. In low tones, I bent over Tadek. 'Tadek,' he didn't move.

' Tadek,' I said a bit louder. He looked up with red rimmed eyes. I sensed his sadness. 'Are you two coming to have our group photo taken? Something to send home; you know, show them you're OK, ' I said persuasively and in a jolly tone. Wojtek stood up and Tadek got up with him. He folded his letter, put it into his shirt pocket and sighed. Great, I thought, success! I smiled at both of my buddies and said in brisk tones, 'Right, we'd better move, or Henio will go spare!'

The three of us joined the others, who were vying for the best seats on the bench. Wojtek ignored protocol and plonked himself heavily right in the middle of the seat, causing it to vibrate. 'Hey! Wojtek get on the ground mate!'

'Where are we going to sit?' Wojtek stayed where he was and the amazing thing is, that he actually sat like one of us on the bench! He was a fast learner and quickly copied any new type of behaviour demonstrated. 'The prof', sat on one side of him, Tadek on the other and the rest of us either squeezed onto the bench, sat on the dusty ground just in front of it, or stood behind these two rows.

Stas appeared munching on a corned beef sandwich, just as Henio was about to take the photograph. He hadn't bargained on Wojtek's presence and was just about to cram the rest of it into his mouth when our bear suddenly got up and made to grab it out of Stas's grasp. As he did so, the bench went flying and so did we!

It was too much for flustered Henio in the heat of the afternoon sun and he threw his hands in the air, releasing a torrent of words I cannot possibly repeat on this page. A couple of soldiers picked up the wooden seat and we resumed our positions; all except for Stas, who went back to the kitchen tent in a huff for more snacks. Wojtek licked his lips as he too sat down again next to his friends.

Henio still looked stressed, so Irek threw him over a half used packet of cigarettes. 'Hey, Henio, relax!' Henio lit a filter – tip and inhaled slowly, then breathed out the smoke. As he did so, Wojtek decided to get off the bench and dropped to all fours on the ground. He went up to Henio and sat in silence, staring at him. Henio stared back and said teasingly holding the cigarette above the bear, 'I suppose you want to try one of *these* now do you Misiu?' Wojtek lifted his snout up, sniffing the nicotine filled air above him; then before Henio could move his hand away, he jumped up and swiped the cigarette out of Henio's grasp, picked it up off the ground, shoved it into his mouth and swallowed it. Henio stared disbelievingly at Wojtek. His hand was still outstretched, his mouth open. For once, Henio was speechless and he wasn't the only one.

We all sat in silent amazement for a few seconds, before Peter, who had been standing behind the bench waiting for the picture to be taken and was alarmed at what had just occurred, ran round to Wojtek to check if he was hurt. After all, he had actually just swallowed an almost whole lit cigarette!

He was really annoyed with Henio. 'Are you mad Private? What on earth do you think you're doing?' Henio stood still, looking quite upset. He just muttered 'Sorry, sir.'

Yet Wojtek seemed unfazed by either the 'fire stick' he had just eaten, or Peter's concern. He allowed his 'mother' to gently prise open his enormous jaws and after a thorough look inside Wojtek's mouth, Peter stood up with a puzzled expression on his face, scratched his head and said 'I don't understand. I mean, thank goodness he's alright, he doesn't seem to have burnt his mouth or anything. I hope his throat's fine as well. I suppose we won't really know that until he's tried to eat something now. He's not in any obvious pain, not groaning or growling or anything.'

We had to agree and tried to reassure Peter. Wojtek 'smiled', rolled over on the ground, shook the dust off himself onto everybody close to him, then went back to his seat, in no apparent discomfort.

That was Wojtek's first experience of a cigarette. He would enjoy hundreds more over the years, but only lit ones. If he was offered any that weren't, even whole ones, he would simply throw them away. He was becoming more and more 'one of the lads', constantly endearing himself to us in unexpected new ways.

Henio, his spirits recovered, focussed the camera on our happy group. We were laughingly discussing Wojtek's latest 'trick'. He meanwhile, ever the showman, sat amongst his dear friends, his family, opened his mouth and grinned directly at the lens. He was like a seasoned model readily posing for yet another picture.

Henio squinted as he called out, 'Right everyone, look this way and say, 'We love Wojtek!' Our enthusiastic response followed by a loud cheer said it all.

* * *

'Wojtek sitting pretty.'

CHAPTER 9

We receive our orders & Wojtek is officially enlisted

It was a bright December morning in 1943. Major Chelkowski stood in front of us in his crisp, spotless uniform; back straight, his gaze steady, unsmiling. Captain Kipiniak solemn faced, positioned himself next to the Major. The latter cleared his throat. 'I have received orders this morning gentlemen, from General Anders himself.' I held my breath, guessing what was coming. I was right. 'Gentlemen, we are to move to Egypt next month, where our Company is to join the Polish 2nd. Corps with the General himself and other British forces. From there, we will set sail for Italy. ' He paused for a moment, scanning the assembled group standing silently, expectantly, in front of him. 'Gentlemen, we will be fighting at Monte Cassino.'

Fingers of fear crept down our backs. A chill went right through me. 'Of course, you all understand that in any correspondence to your loved ones, you are obviously forbidden to mention anything at all about these orders and our movements,' continued the Major. ' Indeed, you must be aware that your letters will be scrutinised even more closely, for the safety of our Company and also that of the other troops involved. This is very sensitive information and it is imperative that it does not fall into the wrong hands.' In other words, our letters would be censored in case anyone was careless enough to reveal any confidential details of our manoeuvres. Bolek and I looked at each other. This was it.

From that day, our Company was more subdued. The raucous laughing, joking and story telling that had been enjoyed around relaxing camp fires on most evenings during our stay in or near the Middle Eastern deserts, became a more muted affair with some talk of the challenges ahead, accompanied by nervous smoking.

I would smoke like a chimney for the rest of my life. It was a habit that is now so frowned upon for obvious reasons and quite rightly so. Nowadays, my children hate it. They keep lecturing me on the evils of a 'roll up' and they may well have a point. However, one never knows what one will do to cope with hardships. You didn't bother about the effects of nicotine at the time, when you were about to risk your life in a battle.

So we took down our tents, packed all of our equipment, provisions and belongings onto jeeps and trucks and headed for Egypt.

Wojtek came with us of course and it was only when we arrived in the port of Alexandria, that Peter mentioned his concerns as to whether the Polish army hierarchy would allow a bear to cross the waters with us to Italy. After all, we were going there to fight. I suppose that because Wojtek had been with us for so long we considered him to be one of us and so it hadn't even occurred to us that he might be stopped from going with our Company to Italy. Our hearts sank, but we never were defeatist. We promised Peter that we would do everything in our power for Wojtek to come with us. We begged Captain Kipiniak and Major Chelkowski to do all they could.

As it happened, Lance Corporal Prendys had the

support of his immediate superior officers and after much calm but persistent entreating from them to the top brass, at the very last minute Wojtek was actually enlisted. He could formally keep his name and was officially given the rank of Private, with his own unique number and a special travel warrant. We were all overjoyed, none more so than Peter Prendys.

On February 13th. 1944, *MS Batory* was waiting for us at the quayside in Alexandria. This was the converted troop ship that would take us to our destiny. I felt nervous, apprehensive, excited, all at once. Bolek was very quiet. The raw, salty smell of the greenish blue sea would forever in my mind be associated with this journey into the dangerous unknown, regardless of however many seaside holidays my family and I would take in the future.

A moving line of trucks and jeeps boarded the impressive looking ship. There in the back of Peter's vehicle smiling broadly, was Private Wojtek.

※ ※ ※

CHAPTER 10

Operation Diadem

Towards the end of April, 1944, the Polish 2nd. Corps and our 22nd. Company arrived at Cassino, the town at the foot of an impressively large mountain. At the top was an ancient, historic Benedictine Abbey.

This would be the scene of one of the bloodiest and perhaps most controversial land battles fought in Europe during the war. It was in fact the toughest, most powerful point of Hitler's Gustav Line, which stretched right across Italy, coast to coast and was being defended by fifteen divisions of the German army. The Allies needed to get past this point so as to achieve their next military objective; of getting to Rome, less than one hundred miles away. There had already been three failed Allied attempts from January that year, to destroy the strong German defensive planted along this rugged mountain terrain and to capture the huge, 1400 year old Abbey situated on its peak.

This time, for the final assault, General Anders had volunteered the 2ND. Polish Army Corps to spearhead this mission, which was to be under British command and known as 'Operation Diadem'.

Polish Infantry alone was to advance right to the top of the rugged mountain on foot to take over the Abbey, whilst other Allied troops including those from Britain, America, South Africa and New Zealand would also be strategically placed for battle in this fourth and decisive assault, though not on the mountain itself. For this reason, they would obviously not be facing the front line as directly as the Polish soldiers who would eventually storm the Abbey. Allied bombers would give all the support they could from the skies above Monte Cassino.

The Royal Engineers, Black Watch, troops from the French Expeditionary Corps and from India would be engaged in other strategic and victorious battles on the Gustav Line.

Our Company was to be responsible for supplying artillery to the Polish and British guns at Monte Cassino and also essential food supplies. In fact after this ultimate siege was over, someone calculated that we actually managed to supply approximately 17320 tons of ammunition; 1200 tons of fuel and 1116 tons of food for these troops.

Strategy Operation Diadem was a bold one, but extremely dangerous, as the Germans had skilfully hidden themselves in concrete bunkers and foxholes all along the mountain side, with their heavy artillery poised and ready. They had also planted mines and barbed wire. They might have been greatly outnumbered, but they somehow managed to hold their positions strongly. Since the assaults had taken place earlier on that year, the mountain had become impenetrable partly for these reasons, but also because of the ruination of the once accessible roads leading to it from nearby Cassino and those on the mountain that led to the Abbey itself. The easiest way to travel this route was by donkey and in fact these wonderful creatures were also used to transport necessary supplies. The formerly smooth tracks were now covered in rubble; stones and rocks lying in between burnt out bushes and trees; dotted here and there were parts of overturned Allied supply trucks that must have misjudged their distance whilst navigating the precarious bends, or had been blown up by the enemy.

Thus our 22nd. Company was given the responsibility of somehow making the hazardous journey through all of these obstacles, including proceeding up part of the treacherous mountainside in order to supply ammunition and food provisions to the men of the Polish 2nd Corps in their artillery positions, who had dug themselves in foxholes of their own, preparing for battle. One of our tasks was therefore to somehow manoeuvre our heavy trucks laden with shells quietly and unobserved over these dirt tracks, including hairpin bends, amidst the enemy, to our men. We had to do this for three weeks before the final assault. It seemed a lot longer.

To say this was a nerve wracking task was an understatement. Clearly, we didn't want to alert the enemy, thus our missions were carried out under cover of darkness, another hazard to contend with. Henio volunteered to drive the first time, though not without some trepidation.

His usual carefree disposition was replaced with a new gravity. 'Someone will have to walk in front as I can't use any lights on the truck, or I don't know how I'm going to get through,' he stated to Major Chelkowski. The Major looked at us. 'Any volunteers?' Irek didn't hesitate. He raised his hand saying, 'I'll go with Henio. I'll walk in front.' What this meant was, that he would be walking slowly right in front of the truck with a light coloured piece of clothing or towel placed around his shoulders, as a guide for Henio. There would have to be total trust between the men and resolute concentration. If either made a mistake, there was the very real possibility that the truck along with all the ammunition it was carrying, would go careering down the mountainside. We had been told horror stories of this having occurred to other supply vehicles since the assaults on Monte Cassino began earlier that year. Not only that, but ostensibly it would also alert the Germans to our activities. Irek drew one last long puff off his cigarette, then took it out of his mouth, threw it on the ground and pressed it into the dirt with his foot before he went to get ready.

I said I would sit in the front with Henio and help with unloading the items when we had reached the Polish soldiers awaiting our arrival. Bolek immediately said he would also go and when I worriedly protested he simply said, 'Brother sticks with brother. We look out for each other, remember? We promised Mum and Dad.' I still felt apprehensive, but couldn't really argue with that, so I just asked him to be careful. Surprisingly, Stas climbed into the back of the truck. ' Someone has to keep an eye on you lot,' he uttered. Henio stared at him, then went up to him and put his arm around Stas's shoulder with, 'Thank you my friend. Thank you Stas. You're a good man.' Stas beamed.

Henio started the engine quietly and we proceeded up the steep track in the silent darkness. It wasn't pitch black, as the waxing moon was half way to fullness, which was useful to us, though we hoped it wouldn't provide any advantage for the enemy. Irek, with a pale cream towel round his neck, walked slowly just slightly ahead, keeping exactly the correct distance from our truck and Henio's eyes were totally focussed on him. Henio looked calm, but I noticed beads of perspiration glistening tellingly on his forehead. His hands were clenching the steering wheel so hard you could see the whites of his knuckles, even in that faint light. We were all nervous, but determined to get the provisions through. Men's lives could depend on the success of our mission.

The rest of us on the truck peered into the darkness all around for any sign of the enemy, guns held tightly in our hands, ready. According to our ordnance instructions, the first Polish artillery positions were placed camouflaged, with their weapons, just after the third bend in the road.

As Irek turned at an angle, we thought great! One bend down, two to go.

We continued for a little while, the engine barely audible as Henio carefully followed Irek. He turned again. We had reached the second bend. Then out of nowhere appeared clouds of 'smoke', dense enough for us to have trouble distinguishing Irek in front. For about thirty tense seconds, only his towel was visible. Strangely, the foggy clouds didn't actually smell of smoke, just sort of musty. 'Great', whispered Henio, sounding frustrated. 'What is it?' asked Bolek in muted tones.

'Artificial fog', answered Henio softly. 'Our people use it to stop the Germans from seeing us. It's useful in one way, but it's even harder for us drivers to see where we're going! Still, it shows we're close now.'

We waited for a few seconds as the smoke dispersed, then Irek began walking cautiously in front again, until he turned a third time. Suddenly, he stopped abruptly. There was the sound of rustling and we automatically cocked our guns, holding our breath. Nothing. Eerie stillness. That's the first time in my life I ever really tasted fear.

Stas hissed, 'Look over there!' he pointed his gun at some bushes on Irek's left, as they shook more violently in the darkness. Irek moved towards them.

'No!' called out Henio quietly, but urgently. However, Irek carried on walking towards the disturbance. My heart was hammering hard in my chest. I hardly dared to breathe. As I watched courageous Irek, a couple of men wearing Polish 2nd. Corps uniforms, jumped out from behind the bushes with their rifles slung over their shoulders. 'At last! We've been waiting for you guys. Have you got the ammo and food?' they enquired in hushed voices. Relief flooded through us, so much so that we wanted to laugh and had to cover our mouths just in case, whilst our eyes looked joyfully at our Polish comrades. 'Hey guys, what's the joke?' they asked in lowered tones.

'Henio just managed to gasp, 'Lets unload the truck,' whilst the rest of us said prayers of thanks under our breath.

The soldiers helped us to unload the supplies of food and artillery, then we in turn helped carry them behind the trees and bushes, to where a group of about ten other men were well hidden in a long, narrow ditch. I could distinguish large guns protruding on one side. Soldiers were sitting in the fox hole, with their helmet covered heads leaning back as they relaxed with their eyes closed. On seeing our arrival, the men looked up and greeted us with smiles of gratitude and enthusiastic handshakes, but naturally hardly whispered a word, so as not to betray their cover. We mouthed 'God bless', then crept back to our truck and just as noiselessly made our way back to our base. I can't describe how we felt on arriving back there safely.

I should explain how Wojtek coped with the trauma of being brought to a real war zone. Initially, he hated it. The alien sounds of loud and frequent gunfire and explosions frightened him terribly and he would run to Peter for comfort and reassurance, whining and whimpering. He had no inclination to explore at all. He wouldn't go anywhere. We'd never seen him like this before and felt quite sorry for him. Whenever the opportunity arose, we would talk to him calmly and give him reassuring hugs.

Then somehow he just seemed to adapt, as if it had never bothered him in the slightest. He would climb up a tall tree near to where we were stationed and observe the action on the enemy lines, no longer bothered by the noises of heavy artillery and bombs.

It was in the middle of such a maelstrom of action that Wojtek surprised us yet again. In fact, his actions now would make him a legend.

The final, decisive assault on Monte Cassino began on 11th. May, 1944. We were under consistently heavy enemy fire for eight days. Since the beginning of this onslaught, we did our best to load and unload heavy boxes and sacks of ammunition and food as quickly as possible to the foot of the mountain. Wojtek sat near to one of the trucks, watching us. Fortunately, the deafening noise didn't seem to bother him anymore.

On one occasion, Irek was just about to hand me a large box of shells, when all of a sudden Wojtek stood up onto his hind legs and came over to where I was standing, with his large paws outstretched next to me, to be given a box to carry just like the rest of us. Irek looked at both of us briefly and I nodded. Without a word, he placed the box into Wojtek's 'arms'. To our utter amazement, Wojtek took the heavy box of ammunition and carried it to one of the trucks, just like he'd observed us do on so many occasions. 'Well done Wojtek!' we shouted over the gunfire and exploding bombs.

Bouyed up by the praise, Wojtek went back to Irek

for another container, grinning broadly. When he had finished unloading that one, he was given a bottle of beer as a reward.

Astonishingly, Wojtek helped us to carry vital supplies in this way day after day, until our Polish brothers took the Monte Cassino Abbey itself. However, Wojtek seemed to decide how long his 'shifts' would be and sometimes after carrying the shells for a while, he would just sit down and not move, content to observe us instead. Until that is, a snack or bottle of beer were waved under his nose for encouragement, when he would then enjoy the tasty treat, get up and continue his work. To his credit, our dear, clever bear never dropped a single shell or any food. He had truly become a soldier and a special one at that. Private Wojtek was a hero.

Allied bombers relentlessly targeted the mountainside, whilst the ground troops and Germans fired their guns savagely at each other. The drone of the planes seemed to be never ending and the heavy bombs they dropped all around us made our hearts leap every time they erupted. Debris and dust flew everywhere. The deadly missiles were frighteningly loud, like enormous thunderclaps right above our heads, temporarily deafening us. The sound of grenades being detonated joined in the orchestra of terror and destruction. Every so often you could hear men screaming in agony and others desperately shouting orders.

Apparently, so we were later told by the airmen, it was bright and sunny during the day, but for the whole time, we didn't see the beautiful sun or blue skies above us. We were trapped in a frightening, grey, misty world, filled with dense, disgusting smelling smoke that stung our eyes and filled our lungs, making us cough, splutter and choke. It was quite a surreal time; like being actors in a science fiction film on some parallel plane in unearthly conditions. Only this was real.

Throughout all this, our brave Polish Infantry somehow climbed on foot to the top of the mountain, to what was left of the once imposing Abbey, which now lay in fragmented pieces everywhere. The heroic soldiers made their way through bullet ridden, bloodied, dead bodies from both sides scattered around, sprawled over rocks, boulders or burning trees; or limbs separated from soldier's bodies visible amongst the remains of destruction. Helmets and caps that had blown off from what were now smouldering corpses lay at a distance from their owners. War is very ugly and the horrors are such that although at the time we are given strength to do our duty whilst enduring the unimaginable, afterwards in peace time it is too painful and horrible to re live all the sheer sickening terror and what was witnessed.

Now you might understand why many veterans don't speak much about their experiences in the war. In years to come, my children, nieces and nephews would ask me to discuss what I did in the war and how I felt and were baffled that I would hardly comment. It wasn't that I wouldn't. I couldn't. I hope they never have to find out why for themselves. It is vital to remember the fallen; the extent of their sacrifice. However, I think it is unwise to dwell on the gruesome pictures of carnage and total fear that are always there at the back of our minds, tucked away in some corner amidst happier images of our lives during the peace we enjoyed before and after the time of trial and test of faith.

Rubble covered the rough tracks we had followed with our trucks for all those weeks and parts of the monastery walls, architecture and statues that had been blown from their home lay in shattered pieces here and there.

At least the antique and invaluable relics and papers from the Abbey's archives in their deep vaults had been saved before the mountain had even been occupied by the Germans. Fortunately (and I say that because just about all the Poles were Catholics) the Nazis had agreed that such contents would be safely transported under their guard and accompanied by chosen monks from the Abbey to the Vatican. Of course, the Germans made such concessions to the Italians because they were allies at the time.

Thus after eight days of constant bombardment and gunfire, on May 18th. 1944, our heroic, exhausted Polish comrades reached the remains of the Abbey on top of the mountain. Only the west wall of the once imposing building was left intact, though its white stone was left damaged and dirtied.

The Polish soldiers were met by the serene face of a beautiful Virgin Mary gazing peacefully down at them, standing intact on one side of the wall. Somehow, astoundingly, this beautifully carved symbol of love had been saved from the flying and exploding bombs and heavy artillery. The soldiers immediately saw this as a sign and at the same time spotted a tattered white flag of surrender being waved by the Germans. So with renewed courage and a last blast of vigour, they stormed what was left of the Abbey itself. Within a short time, they triumphantly led out a number of German soldiers at gunpoint that had been hiding there. The Poles escorted them, their arms high above their heads in surrender, through the terrible devastation to other Polish soldiers further down the mountain. The wounded Germans were carried out on stretchers by their countrymen.

Meanwhile, the Polish flag was planted firmly,

thankfully on top of the mountain, by what was left of Monte Cassino Abbey. The soldiers stood next to it for a while, praying. They thanked God and Poland's patron, the Virgin Mary for keeping them alive and for the ferocious fighting to have come to an end.

All at once the bombing, firing and explosions ceased. The Allied troops had quickly received word of the German surrender and they had also seen the Polish standard raised at the top of the mountain. The filthy, suffocating smoke settled and the branches of innocent trees quietly burned all around. We waited. Just to make sure. Then out of the new divine peace, the haunting sounds of the Polish bugler sounding the Hejnal could be heard floating over the mountain side. It was over. More than a week of long, laborious, exhausting, frightening, heavy fighting and appalling casualties had finally reached their conclusion.

Bolek and I and all the other men hugged each other, sobbing so hard we couldn't speak. The long, gruelling, sleepless days and nights had taken their toll on everyone. Wojtek joined in, sensing the depth of emotion. He also wanted a cuddle. Then we said prayers of thanksgiving.

I was so grateful that my brother and my friends including dear Wojtek, were safe, thank God. Unfortunately, the same could not be said for so many others who fell whilst leading or helping their Allied comrades. The 2nd Corps itself suffered 1150 losses and 4199 casualties.

The fighting continued along other parts of the Gustav Line until eventually the Germans were decisively forced to retreat by the Allies.

Sadly, there were huge numbers of British and Allied casualties here also.

The verdict to honour Wojtek's actions during the

lengthy siege was unanimous. We even observed that intriguingly, his temperament after Monte Cassino was just the same as it had always been, despite what we had all experienced. Thus one of the soldiers drew a picture of our furry, fearless brother carrying an artillery shell, with a steering wheel in the background to highlight the fact that he was part of a transport Company.

This was made into a badge which on 14th. February, 1945 (what an appropriate date!) officially became the 22nd. Company's insignia and was proudly worn by all of us, including other Poles, on our uniforms. I recall the first time we got them. Peter was thrilled; he looked like a delighted, honoured parent. In fact, Wojtek's military logo appeared everywhere; even on military equipment. When Bolek and I were eventually reunited with the rest of our family after the war, my younger sister asked why we had a badge with a bear on it sewn onto my regulation army shirt sleeve. She and thousands of other Polish families and for generations to come, would be told the legend of Wojtek.

The assault's objective had been achieved. The road to Rome was open. This age old city would fall to the Allies in June, leading to the D-Day invasion. There would be no real respite from the trials of battle for some time to come, as we travelled with the 2nd.Corps along the Adriatic coast to Ancona, which was captured in July, 1944. Finally, we all reached Bologna in April, 1945 and after a fierce battle, captured it from the Germans. In May. 1945, Germany surrendered, signalling the end of the long, weary war. Peace at last.

* * *

CHAPTER 11

Holiday in Italy

The next few months felt like an exhilaratingly happy summer holiday after the trauma and atrocities of war. It was as if we had awoken from a terrible nightmare into a haven of joy and peace.

Our Company remained near the picturesque Adriatic coast, enjoying sunbathing on the stunning, sandy beaches; our bare feet stepping through soft, warm grains of sand – not desert sand this time. There was also the post war Italian hospitality. The feisty, emotional, religious, food and music loving temperament of the people in this balmy, sunny, European climate was actually very similar to that of the Poles. Maybe that was why so many of our Company took Italian brides after the war and why so many of us returned time and time again in later years with our families.

Many was the time elated singing could be heard either outside in the street from open café windows, our trucks or along the shore itself when we'd enjoyed a beer or two in the baking sun. Naturally Wojtek would join in with the socialising. Sometimes we were so relaxed that we lost count of how many beers Wojtek had actually imbibed, until he seemed to have some difficulty in walking in a straight line. He would move slowly, swaying from side to side, grinning. That was one of the signs.

He would also constantly yawn, then sometimes just

lie down wherever he could find any shade and sleep it off, snoring loudly and contentedly.

Alcohol generally had similar effects on him as on a human, although fortunately it never made him aggressive. Obviously we were careful at such times not to allow our party loving bear to go anywhere near the inviting waters of the Adriatic. Someone would always keep a watchful eye over him.

Wojtek of course, was in his element. When he hadn't partaken of any alcohol, he loved swimming in the warm, welcoming, clear blue Adriatic Sea and would delight in performing his usual trick of swimming underwater for a while, only to surface next to a group of unsuspecting bathers, usually women of course. He really enjoyed female company and attention, just like the rest of us! Of course we weren't the only people playing on the beach; there were also a large number of civilians and the last thing they were expecting to see in the water was a huge Persian bear.

Wojtek of course found the usual screams of panic very amusing and it only encouraged him to continue with his 'game'. We did try to call him back several times, but he turned a deaf ear to our shouts, determined not to move away from his female friends; until that is, one day we were running late for our return to the base.

Peter was urgently calling Wojtek to come back ashore so as to dry him off quickly before we jumped into our trucks. Wojtek acted as though he didn't hear and kept swimming around a small group of young women who were treading water huddled together. We thought they were too scared to try and swim past our lively bear splashing around them. Mind you, we noticed that whilst a few of the girls looked genuinely scared, a couple of them were also looking and smiling in the direction of Peter, Bolek and myself, as we stood on the edge of the shore waving and shouting, attempting to get Wojtek's attention. Maybe some of them weren't so afraid after all!

Bolek and I were just about to wade into the water to see if we would have to swim out to our playful bear, when suddenly we heard the sound of an engine being started behind us. We turned round to look. It was Henio, who had thought of the brilliant idea of pretending to leave the beach and thus see if we would get a reaction from Wojtek.

It was an inspired thought. Wojtek always panicked if we were out somewhere and he thought he would be left behind for some reason. No sooner had Wojtek heard the sound of the engine being revved up behind him, than he turned round, looked in the direction of the waiting trucks and sped out of the water. Peter, Bolek and I laughingly followed him at a more sedate pace.

Wojtek, dripping wet, ran straight up to Peter's truck and shook himself hard. Sea water sprayed everywhere, including Stas who was standing nearby enjoying the sun. 'Oh Wojtek!' he moaned, looking down at his soaking khaki shorts and took off his glasses splattered with sea water to dry them. Peter grinned, grabbed the nearest towel and rubbed Wojtek as dry as he could. 'The sun will do the rest' he commented, squinting at the dazzling light shining through the perfectly clear blue sky.

Wojtek as usual climbed into the passenger seat of Peter's vehicle. It was so hot that the windows were wound down and Wojtek made the most of it, sticking his lovely, large, brown head out, enjoying the warm air blowing through his freshly washed fur. Every so often he would lift his snout up to the gentle breeze, absorbing different smells that filled his nostrils along the journey to the field where we were camped. As we wound our way down the coastal roads, Wojtek's smiling face stared at everything we passed on the way. He took an interest in everything he saw and as always, loved the reaction of bewildered locals stopping in their tracks gaping at him. He really loved being the centre of attention.

At the end of the 'summer holiday' in September 1946, we arrived in Naples, ready for our journey to Glasgow. We were aware that the Russians were doing bad things in our homeland, though we didn't know all of the details as yet. We would find these out gradually in the next few years and also how Poland came to be literally just handed over into Stalin's hands by the Allies with whom we had fought alongside.

At the Yalta conference in February, 1945, Roosevelt and Churchill publicly confirmed their pact with Stalin, agreeing that Poland would remain under Russian occupation. Poland had not been invited to participate in these negotiations. The official line was that Stalin had gained the support of the two Allied leaders, by stating that he would allow free elections in our country. Roosevelt and Churchill readily acquiesced as this suited their plans for a closer partnership with Stalin. They were prepared to offer up Poland to the Soviets like a sacrificial lamb. Our wonderful General Sikorski, who had been Prime Minister for the Polish-Government -In -Exile based in London had sadly died in a plane crash two years earlier over Gibraltar. Perhaps had he still been alive, there would have been less likelihood of this injustice being so easily meted out.

As a result, our dear homeland was coldly, dispassionately carved up like a piece of meat. To say that the Poles felt hurt and betrayed was putting it mildly. The map of Poland was altered, with a large section of eastern Poland being gleefully seized by the Soviets to be now classed as part of their state. Supposedly as a way of recompense, the eastern part of Germany would be added to Polish territory. In fact, Stalin also took control of the rest of Poland, ruling with a despotic fist.

To return home to post war Poland was either impossible due to this dreadful Communist regime ruling our country with an iron grip, or would have meant a lifetime of oppression or suffering; many who did return being sent to cruel, inhumane Siberian labour camps, often never to be heard of again. A similar fate awaited those who dared to oppose the new edict.

The least the Allies could now do after putting us in this position and particularly after our war effort was to offer us a safe haven. Don't get me wrong. We were and are very grateful for being allowed to stay either here in Britain or other countries that were willing to take us. But you understand our feelings. Over the years, one learns to forgive, but the scars of mistrust remain.

Many Poles felt wounded by the ease with which they were 'sold' to the Soviets by seemingly uncaring Allied powers, particularly after Poland's tremendous sacrifices fighting alongside these countries. Even the fact that heroic Polish squadrons led important and dangerous missions during the Battle Of Britain appeared to have been completely ignored until recently. Why, we don't know, or why Polish troops weren't allowed to parade with others through London in the Victory Parade after the war ended. It's as if attempts were made to wipe out our role and sacrifices in the war.

What we did know at the time however, was that we

were now being transported to Britain because Stalin was worried about the quarter of a million patriotic Polish soldiers returning to their country bearing a strong hatred for the Soviet Communist dictatorship that continued to crush it.

Stalin saw us as a threat he didn't want.

Consequently, freedom from the war had come at a painful price. For our country, there was to be no freedom from this tyrannical dictatorship for over thirty years, until by the grace of God, Solidarity peacefully liberated Poland from its oppressors.

Initially, after Churchill signed the ominous agreement with Stalin, the British government wanted to send the Polish 'Government – In –Exile' back to Poland to participate in the so called new elections promised by the Soviet dictator. However, when they were informed that Stalin had already established an interim government which would in effect be totally under Soviet rule and news of persecution and atrocities filtered through, the British had to rethink their decision. In addition, thousands of Polish soldiers and their families would now be unable to return to their homeland.

So it happened that we were on our way to Scotland. We were hopeful that our arrival in a totally unfamiliar country would somehow turn out to have positive consequences. We felt rested and replenished after our lengthy Italian 'vacation', which helped boost our sense of optimism. We were also overjoyed at the thought of being reunited with our families after such a long period of separation, though that too would not happen for nearly two more long years. In 1948, my family would also be transported by ship from Africa to the U.K. Eventually, we soldiers would be demobbed and have the choice of either risking our lives by going back to Poland with our loved ones which a relatively small number did; staying in Britain, or moving to the U.S, Canada, Argentina, Australia or New Zealand to begin a new life in peaceful exile.

I have to say that in addition to twinges of excitement, we also felt slightly apprehensive at the thought of arriving in Scotland; a country that was virtually unknown to us. What was it like? How did people live? Did they speak in English? How would the people there react to us? Where would we live? So many questions! In a little while they would be answered.

✷ ✷ ✷

CHAPTER 12

New Beginnings

We were touched by the warmth of the waving, cheering crowds, as our Company marched through the city of Glasgow in the pleasant September sunshine. Our morale and optimism for the future were high. Wojtek loved being centre stage. To squeals of delight from the multitude of people lining the streets, every so often his impressive frame would stretch itself to full height on his hind legs and he would wave his large paws, before dropping back onto all fours.

Our theatrical celebrity basked in the warm glow of love from the Scottish people. He was of course walking next to Peter and when Wojtek ambled along on the ground, Peter would place his hand on his shoulder, protectively and proudly. As I glanced back at them, I thought it looked like a circus had come to town!

We were to stay temporarily in a transit camp nearby, until we were moved to Winfield Camp in the Borders, on 28th. October, 1946 and what beautiful countryside it was. However, soon after we arrived at our new home in Berwickshire, reality set in.

This was 'Spartan Tartan' post war Scotland. People had to live frugally, as there was still rationing during this period. We managed, though at first we were a bit concerned as to how we would feed Wojtek, as this huge cuddly bear needed a massive number of calories to sustain him. This was especially relevant in the coming winter months, when brown bears tended to put on weight in preparation for hibernation. As it happened, Wojtek only semi-hibernated, as he was being constantly fed and he still participated at least in part to activities with his Polish comrades. It was as though he was disregarding what would have been behaviour natural to his kind and instead continuing to emulate that of his human brothers.

As it was, we needn't have worried about his diet, for very kind local country folk started regularly popping into the camp with provisions donated from their own rations. I will always remember their benevolence. Some would pop in to check if we needed anything and would then stay for a good while talking to Wojtek and sharing beer or cigarettes with him. Children loved Wojtek and had great fun riding on his back. No 'health and safety police' then!

So Wojtek was a major attraction and once people nearby discovered he was tame, did tricks and loved any snacks, would drop in whenever they could. It tended to be the same people and Wojtek learnt to recognise those who always brought tasty treats for him, such as bacon, apples, bread, eggs and honey. He would reward their generosity with his trademark smile, standing on his hind legs and then roll over on the ground. It always had the desired effect. Soon afterwards, he was guaranteed another visit from the same visitors and more snacks.

There was one occasion when for some reason, Wojtek had missed his morning brunch; delicious honey sandwiches. It was still another hour until lunch. For this reason, he was feeling very hungry and had been stalking the cookhouse for a good while already, getting more and more frustrated, when Bolek and I on returning from our duties, approached him.

He had sat himself down right in front of one of the small, open windows of the vast hut, sniffing the air which was filled with the mouth watering aromas of frying bacon and fresh, baking bread. How he wished he could get into the cookhouse! That wasn't so easy since the last time he had broken into it about a week ago.

The four young ladies from a nearby village who came regularly to help our cook Marian with the main meals, had decided to go for a walk around the camp during their morning break. Meanwhile Marian had gone to see the Captain for a few minutes. That was all it took.

The door of the cookhouse had been left slightly ajar and Wojtek, always on the look out for food, had jumped at the opportunity to enter the 'forbidden zone'. There were baskets of bread and fruit on a trestle table, so he helped himself to 'pawfuls' of these as he continued exploring the rest of this tempting, fascinating area filled with the most scrumptious food. As he walked past the table, he accidentally knocked a large box of freshly laid eggs and they fell with audible cracks; gooey yellow and white liquid oozing over part of the polished floor. Wojtek continued his hunt for refreshments and helped himself to a plate of tasty ready made chicken sandwiches. Without hesitation, he sat down to enjoy them and the rest of his unexpected feast.

After a few minutes, there was the sound of girly chatter as the young women entered the hut, slightly surprised to see the door wide open and then screams as they saw the back of Wojtek's huge, furry frame sitting on the floor, happily munching away, making the sort of noises bears do when they are really enjoying a meal and finally showing his appreciation with a resounding burp. Until now, the girls had only seen our bear from a distance and had been quite afraid of him because of his size, even though they had been told he was harmless and had witnessed some of his antics from afar.

Their screeching surprised Wojtek and he swiftly tried to get up onto his hind legs. As he did so, he slipped on the slimy mess on the floor and landed just near the girls. More yelling as they ran out of the cookhouse. After that incident and a sound reprimand from Peter, the door to the cookhouse was locked, much to Wojtek's disappointment.

Thus, as he was presently being denied taking advantage of the kitchen produce as one of his favourite pastimes, he felt the need to indulge himself in another; scratching his back with a branch he had broken off from a nearby tree. A bear had to amuse himself somehow whilst awaiting his next meal.

Actually, as you walked around the camp boundaries, you would often come across discarded branches here and there, broken off and dropped haphazardly. He would also snack on the surrounding vegetation whenever he felt a bit peckish, including trees, bushes and berries. Really, it was a wonder none of the neighbours complained. I think the locals were very tolerant really. Wonderful people.

Wojtek frequently practised his habit of scaling trees for snacks and also to provide for himself another form of entertainment, of studying the local countryside. He either did the latter from a height, or sat for a good while on the ground, staring totally absorbed and fascinated at the wildlife, including rabbits, foxes and birds. He never hurt them.

We sat ourselves on the freshly shorn grass next to him. 'What's the matter fella?' I asked, as my brother and I fondled his soft ears. Wojtek liked this. He stopped scratching, throwing the branch he had held in his paw behind him, grinned and enveloped us in a big, gentle hug. We were just about to sit down next to him, when we heard voices. Visitors!

To Wojtek that meant snacks. He didn't hesitate. You never saw him move so fast as when he got a whiff of food. Before we could stop him, he darted round the back of the huts on all fours and straight to the gate of our camp enclosure.

'Wojtek, wait!' we shouted, as we ran after him. Too late. Wojtek's strong sense of smell zoomed in on the middle aged lady's straw shopping bag, just as she was opening it for our friend Tadek. She had been chatting away animatedly with him, both trying to make themselves understood by the other, when she heard heavy footsteps running behind her, followed by loud panting and then hot breath on her neck. She spun round and seeing over zealous Wojtek standing upright in front of her, screamed at such volume she could be heard all over the camp and probably by her husband at their farm next door!

Wojtek stood on his hind legs, snatched her bag with one of his huge, brown paws and threw it on the ground. Four white, shiny, hard boiled eggs rolled out. The woman screamed again and ran off at speed through the gate and down the country lane, abandoning her bag on the ground.

Wojtek picked up the eggs, sat down and stuffed them into his mouth, all at the same time. Then he leaned over, took the bag in his paws and tipped it upside down. When only a handkerchief floated out, he watched it for a few seconds as it gently descended to the ground, then peered inside, sniffing the bag to see if there were anything else more interesting - that is, edible, hiding inside.

The three of us tried to admonish Wojtek, but we

couldn't stop laughing. It didn't help that Wojtek began playing the clown and standing up on his hind legs still clutching his new 'toy', until the handles slipped down one of his 'arms'. He folded his arm inwards like women do when they carry handbags. Bolek and I were rolling around on the grass, laughing so much it hurt. Wojtek was smilingly turning round first in one direction, then the other, as if he was dancing and the more we hooted and screamed, the more he played up to it.

At this point, Peter Prendys arrived, his face like thunder. He stared at Wojtek, then at us and at first the expression on his face made us giggle even more. However, our Lance Corporal didn't appear to see the funny side of the incident. Rather, he was like an irate parent about to give his child a very firm telling off. That's exactly what he did. In fact, I had never witnessed Peter reprimanding Wojtek so severely. 'How DARE you, Wojtek! What do you think you are doing? Look how you frightened that poor woman. I saw her running away. BAD bear. GREEDY bear. We give you more than enough food and you get extras from other people. If you want those people to *keep* bringing you snacks, you MUST behave.' Peter didn't shout, but spoke loudly, slowly and deliberately, emphasising certain words for effect. Wojtek sat down and stared mournfully at his angry guardian.

'You treat guests who visit this camp with respect, do you hear me? Don't ever do that again.' Wojtek looked at his 'parent' sheepishly, dropping onto all fours. As he did so, the bag dropped to the ground. '

'Now go to your hut. You will be tethered for a while to teach you a lesson. Come with me. '

Bolek and I stood quietly. The fact that Peter was so upset had calmed us considerably. We wondered if Peter had been maybe a bit too hard on his charge, but later that evening over a cigarette, Peter explained that he was worried in case local people not really understanding Wojtek's behaviour, might campaign for him to be removed from Winfield, imagining him to be a danger. Peter was right. We were new here, in a foreign country. *We* knew how gentle and harmless our huggable bear was and his habits; locals didn't to the same extent as yet and there was still the problem of the language barrier.

Wojtek sensed that Peter meant business and wasn't in the mood to be brought round by rolling on the floor, so he didn't even try. He hung his head in shame and slowly walked towards his quarters (yes, he had his own hut) next to Peter's, looking very sorry for himself. Peter strode on ahead purposefully, his face flushed and mouth tightly closed. He didn't speak to Wojtek again until he untethered him at teatime. Our loveable, comical bear didn't like upsetting his dear Peter. He had learnt his lesson. Later that evening, Peter was grooming him as usual outside his hut before retiring and when he had finished, Wojtek licked him lovingly on his face, before receiving a gentle pat on the head.

✲ ✲ ✲

'Nearly there…'

CHAPTER 13

What *did you say?*

The men of our 22nd. Company had faced many perils during the war, but had not bargained for the less dangerous though still quite fraught problems concerning language.

We had learnt a few phrases since our arrival a couple of months ago and the amenable locals had also made an effort to use a few words in Polish, such as 'Good morning' or 'Good evening'; 'Please' and 'Thank you'. Anything other than that and good old sign language was generally used by all concerned.

A story that has been related by all of us to our families in later years with much hilarity, concerns a shopping trip made by Henio to a greengrocer's in the nearby village soon after arriving at Winfield. Our cook Marian was in need of a few bags of flour. Peter was grooming Wojtek and the rest of us were carrying out our camp duties. It so happened that Henio had just finished his and had announced that he was going to the popular sweetshop just next door to the grocer's, so he was asked to fetch the required items. He would be reminded of his parting statement, 'No problem' for a long time afterwards.

After spending a little while choosing bags of delicious toffees and mints for the Company, Henio tucked them into his army coat pockets and went next door. A bell rang out loudly, informing the shop assistant that a customer had entered. She was about fifty years of age, small, plump and wearing a floral green and red apron. She finished serving the well dressed woman in front of her, calling 'Thank ye kindly, Mrs. McDougall. I'll have the apples for ye tomorrow!' as the latter turned round with a nod and walked briskly out of the door, sounding the bell again.

Seeing Henio standing near the door, his eyes searching for something, the assistant beckoned for him to come over to the counter. Henio did as he had been bid. The woman's sharp, green eyes peered over glasses that framed her round, pink face. She recognised Henio's uniform. 'Ah, Polish. GOOD MORNING, MY NAME IS MRS. HARRIS, 'she said loudly, like the British do for some strange reason to foreigners. Shouting doesn't actually improve understanding.

Henio had felt a little nervous at having to communicate in English and to be honest, her strong Scottish accent though interesting to listen to, didn't help his dilemma. However, the woman's friendly disposition towards him made him feel more at ease. He attempted, 'Good afternun. How..how..are..YOU?' he managed to say hesitatingly with a distinct Polish accent, feeling very pleased with himself. He watched as a ginger curl escaped from under the green headscarf tying back her hair and bobbed up and down as she spoke.

'Aye, laddie, I'm very well, thank ye. Now young man, what can I get ye?'

There was no way Henio grasped any of that. 'Co?' (What?) he enquired in Polish.

The woman tried again, louder. 'I SAID, WHAT CAN I GET YE?' gesturing to the tins and bags of provisions neatly filling several wooden shelves. It clicked. Henio thought for a moment, staring at the rows and rows of items in front of him. Spotting a small, bulging, brown bag with a picture of a wheat sheaf on the front, situated on the shelf directly behind the shop assistant, he assumed that must be the bag of flour and triumphantly pointed to it, saying excitedly, 'Maka! (*pronounced monka*) 'Maka!'

Mrs. Harris's demeanour changed completely. Her face flushed to the same deep shade of crimson as the flowers on her apron. She stood up straight and stared furiously at unsuspecting Henio. 'How DARE ye!'

Henio froze. He hadn't got a clue what he'd done, but obviously he'd upset this woman in some way. He felt nervous. What *was* she saying?

Unfortunately, he tried to make himself understood by repeating 'Maka'.

This time she started screaming. 'Police! Help! Get the police someone!' The owner of the sweetshop next door ran inside. Meanwhile, the plump greengrocer's assistant carried on screaming. Within two minutes, the tall, uniformed, stoutly built beat bobby had arrived. Mrs. Harris was crying into her apron, pointing at bewildered Henio and sobbing, 'He called me a monkey. That rude Polish soldier called *me* a monkey! I'm *not* a monkey!' She looked despondently at the policeman. 'P.C Fraser, *you* don't think I look like a monkey, do you?' P.C Fraser was trying to work out what was happening. Henio just stood there, looking helplessly at the policeman, arms outstretched in confusion. He was frantically trying to think of the right words.

' How do you say….?Ah, yes.' He looked at the policeman and tried to make himself understood. 'I.. no… .how…you say.. un..der..stand. I no understand! Help me pliz. I vont *maka*!' The shop assistant burst into tears again and moved behind P.C Fraser. Henio darted behind the counter, pointing at the shelf. The policeman began to realize this was no more than a misunderstanding and not an international incident. Henio reached up to the bag of flour, took it off the shelf and held it in front of the policeman. 'Maka. I vont *maka.*'

The policeman stared in turn at Henio holding the bag of flour and then at the red eyed grocer's assistant. He roared with laughter. His guffaws could be heard down the street. Mrs. Harris cautiously came out from behind the policeman. Henio was puzzled, but relieved that he wasn't in trouble with the law. What would his officers at the camp have said? What *was* going on?

After a few minutes, P.C Fraser was calmer, but still chuckling. He cleared his throat, taking the flour out of Henio's grasp. He looked at the woman, who also seemed to have been enlightened as to what had happened. 'Oh, ' she said, sheepishly, looking rather embarrassed. Henio looked at them both enquiringly, though he was now certain he had somehow been let off the hook, whatever he was supposed to have done.

'Look here laddie, ' the enforcer of the law began, trying to keep his face straight, 'Is this what ye were after?' He pointed to the flour. Henio also pointed to it.

'Maka', he said carefully, keeping an eye on the woman's reaction.

'Monka', repeated the policeman. 'Yes!' called out the delighted soldier in relief. 'I nid maka for fud'.

P.C Fraser spoke slowly and clearly. 'Laddie, in this bonny country of ours, we call this fl-ou-r; flour.'

'Yes, maka', said Henio.

'No, flour,' repeated the policeman patiently.

'Aaah.' Henio uttered, illuminated at last. 'Wy lady scrim?'

'Mrs. Harris was a wee bit upset because she thought you were calling her a *monkey.*' Henio furrowed his brow in confusion. 'Maka?' P.C Fraser took a deep breath and rolled his eyes up at the ceiling.

Henio's traumatic experience was enough to make us all ask for English language lessons as soon as possible and for months to come, whenever Henio asked a favour someone would smirk and say, 'No problem.' Needless to say, the next time our cook needed any shopping, we were all far too busy with our duties.

* * *

CHAPTER 14

Winfield Winter Wonderland

Our first winter living in the Winfield Camp was a severe one even by Scottish standards, with temperatures plummeting to over -20°C and very heavy snow. However, we had experienced worse than that in Poland, being an East European country and as such renowned for its particularly freezing winters. Besides, we had survived the harshness of Siberia and you can't get much colder than that.

Nonetheless, there *were* difficult moments that caused a few problems during these bleak weather conditions, only really because our simple, flimsily built Nissan huts had not been adapted for them. They were large and difficult to heat, therefore very cold and damp. Still, it didn't bother Wojtek, who slept more throughout the winter and was happy enough enjoying his long naps in the straw filled hut he had all to himself, whilst being fed in between, groomed by Peter and enjoying the odd activity with us.

Our 'gang' shared one of these huts with fifteen others. There was one morning when it was Irek's turn to get out of his bunk bed first and go to the kitchen hut for Wojtek's breakfast. 'I'll be back in two minutes', he said sleepily and yawning loudly, went to open the hut door.

It wouldn't budge. Being the strongest of course, Irek couldn't understand this and tried again, pushing against the door with all his might. 'Hey, guys!' he called to us sleepy comrades. 'I can't get the door open.'

'*Irek,*' we groaned in unison, Bolek and I pulling the blankets over our heads. 'No, really I can't.' He himself was surprised. We jumped out of our beds, shivering, pulling the covers around us tightly. Peter and Henio stood there barefooted, yawning widely, whilst Stas put on his glasses and joined me at the window. Fine, frozen rivers of intricately patterned ice had formed on the misty window pane. I tried to wipe them off the glass with my hand, but they were set solid. I peeked through a small, unfrozen corner of the window. The view outside was incredibly beautiful, like a fairy tale land. There must have been over ten feet of thick, pure white snow folding over and between the huts, trees and fencing. We gasped at the sight, then turned our attention to the immediate challenge of how we were gong to get out!

A few hours later and our Company had dug their way out of the huts and a path around the camp. After a hearty hot breakfast, we made sure that we dressed suitably and went off with our trusty shovels to clear the neighbouring roads. A number of our Scottish friends turned out to help us and so began even closer ties with the local community.

Wojtek came out to roll around in the newly cleared snow and tread with his big heavy footprints all around, packing more of it together. Everyone laughed and some even tentatively ventured to pat him lightly on his shoulder. There was a very happy atmosphere; faces red with exertion and the cold smiling joyously; misty air exhaled heavily all around with the effort of moving the heavy loads we were shifting.

When the work was finished for the day, we would

throw snowballs at each other; soldiers (with Wojtek) against the Scots. There would be shrieks from both sides as we were 'hit' by a snowball. Wojtek didn't understand at first and bounded around in the deep snow around everyone playfully, pausing every so often to shake his wet, snow covered fur all over whoever he was standing next to at the time. There were moans of *'Oh Wojtek!'* from a number of 'victims'. However, soon every time one of our camp were 'hit', he would rear up on his hind legs and growl at whoever had done the deed. The soldiers knew it was a harmless display, but it was enough to make our Scottish friends more wary of targeting us again, whilst we gave back as good as we got. We had great fun,

Afterwards, true to form, Wojtek helped to carry the shovels back to the camp. The Scots were amazed to see him clutching the tools in his giant paws and walk back with us on his hind legs. I think it was only then that some of them began to believe our stories of his wartime deeds.

They told their friends and families and one day out of the blue, a reporter turned up on the camp's doorstep. Our photo standing with shovels and Wojtek against the snowy background was soon in the local papers. As a consequence, more people learnt of our and Wojtek's presence and it encouraged many more people to visit our camp the following spring. Quite by chance Wojtek and our Company became regional celebrities!

* * *

'Well done Wojtek! Just don't drop it onto my foot!'

CHAPTER 15

Drinking, Dancing, Romancing

There was a good social life in the villages around the camp and we made the most of it. Poles are a sociable lot anyway and don't need an excuse for a song and some dancing. A few men in our Company played musical instruments; Adam on the accordion, Marek played the piano and you could often hear Tomek's harmonica well into the evening from his hut. After Adam and Marek had borrowed a local band's instruments during one lively night out, they were donated their own by a very generous, anonymous benefactor. We just found them outside the camp entrance one morning.

It is a mild spring evening in May that is particularly imprinted on my memory. Most of us were preparing to go to a dance that had been organised by the local parish at the nearby village hall. We Poles like to look smart and were looking forward to meeting some girls, so we spent quite some time getting ready with what resources we had. That is, a good shower, clean uniform and some Brylcreem sleeking down our hair and we were ready for a good time.

Peter was getting ready in his hut, whilst Wojtek sat watching him fascinated, as he opened the large tub of Brylcreem, rubbed it in his hands, then patted it on his thick hair until it looked wet, then combed it carefully. Wojtek dipped his paw into the thick, white cream, put it near his nostrils to smell it, then licked it off with his long, pink tongue. Mmm, very tasty, he thought. He was about to dip his paw in again when it was snatched off him. 'Wojtek, what are you doing? That's not a snack!' exclaimed Peter.

The inquisitive bear simply got up and moved to the mirror, which was only small and balanced on top of Peter's bunk bed. Wojtek placed himself between the mirror and his guardian, making it impossible for the latter to see what he was doing. Our bear stood on his hind legs and just stared at his reflection with a big grin on his lovely face, shifting his weight from one foot to the other. He loved looking at his own image.

'Wojtek, stop admiring yourself in the mirror and let me see what I'm doing will you? It's nearly time to go and I'm not ready. Move will you?' Wojtek didn't budge. 'Wojtek, I know you understand. MOVE!' Still No response from the bear. Peter had a brainwave. He took a dollop of Brylcreem and quickly smoothed it down over the top of Wojtek's furry head, between his ears. Wojtek sniffed the cream above him and tried to wipe some of it off with his paws. As he did so, he moved over to the door and straightaway Peter stepped in front of the mirror, finishing off combing his hair and knotting his tie. Wojtek sat on the floor licking his paw over and over again. Whatever was in the Brylcreem, it definitely appealed to Wojtek!

We shouted for any stragglers and waited a few minutes before jumping into our trucks and heading off to the dance, laughing and joking. Everyone was in a good mood. Naturally, Wojtek came too. There was no way he was going to miss out on the fun!

Entering the large church hall, we were met with suspicious stares from the men, worried about competition for their females and warm smiles from the girls themselves. Some older villagers who were there to ensure there was no trouble to mar the evening's enjoyment (that was how it was done in those days) nodded acknowledgement. Several couples were dancing to a lively Glenn Miller hit, whilst the band of five local lads played with gusto. Our three instrumentalists went straight up to them, partly to watch and also to venture a request for them to be allowed to play a few Polish tunes as well later.

A couple of elderly members of the Parish committee, one of them the vicar's wife and the other a councillor, came up and shook our hands, wishing us a pleasant time. They stared warily at Wojtek, who was actually on his best behaviour and had sat down next to Peter near the doorway. He was eyeing up familiar looking brown beer bottles being swigged by a few raucous men at a table nearby. His eyes sparkled.

Mrs. Andrews, the vicar's wife turned to us. She was well known and respected in the area and helped out regularly at social functions. She was quite tall and very slim, with grey hair pulled back in a neat chignon and dressed in an elegant dark green evening gown, belted at the waist. 'I'm sorry boys, but yer bear will have to stay outside. We canna allow him in here. Ye do understand?'

Mr. Stewart, had been a councillor for over twenty years. He was of small, slight build, with thinning, white hair. He too was smartly dressed in a dark suit and buttoned up waistcoat. Glasses with thin, black frames hung from a thin, silver chain around his neck. As he spoke to us, he perched the glasses on the end of his nose, dark brown eyes peering over them looking a bit stern.

'Aye lads, Mrs. Andrews is right. This is no place for a bear, so it isn't. Best he stays outside.'

Peter spoke very politely. 'Zat is no problem, tank you. Wojtek, hoc (come).' Then turning to us, he said, It's a lovely night. I'll stay with Wojtek boys, don't worry. Just bring us out a couple of beers, won't you?'

'We'll do better than that Peter, we'll take it in turns to stay with him, so that you can enjoy the dance as well', I said. The others nodded in agreement. So Peter and Wojtek went out, while the rest of us went to the bar. After we had bought our drinks, Bolek, Henio, Stas, Jacek, Tadek and myself sat down at a table together, ready to make the most of the evening.

The young men watched us buy our beers and move to different tables. We relaxed and chatted, whilst noticing some attractive, well dressed girls standing close by sipping what looked like lemonade through straws and giving us the eye. A couple more beers later and we might have the courage to approach them, though what we would say to them we didn't know, as our knowledge of English was quite limited. Still, it would be interesting! After an hour or so, the band took a break while Adam, Tomek and Marek took their positions on the stage and began playing a smooth waltz.

Henio had been staring for ages at a sweet looking, dark haired girl aged about eighteen with hair curled down to her shoulders. There was a row of wooden chairs on the other side of the hall, where the single girls sat talking to each other animatedly, trying not to look like they were waiting to be asked for a dance. The object of Henio's desire was sitting next to an equally attractive fair haired friend. When our musicians began to play, he took a deep breath and stood up saying, 'Here goes. Wish me luck boys.' We raised our glasses saying, 'To Henio, na zdrowie! (Cheers!) Good luck!'

The dark haired girl smiled at Henio as he sauntered up to her. Just as he was about to introduce himself, a tall, muscular, local lad in his early twenties and his shorter well built friend of roughly the same age, who had been drinking and watching us from the bar, swiftly went over and placed themselves in between Henio and the girls. 'Do ye want something Pole?' the taller, flame haired, freckled face one said, threateningly. He had a ginger moustache and eyebrows of a similar colour. He obviously liked a drink (or four) as his face was quite red. His nose was the deepest shade. You couldn't help but stare at him, intrigued. We'd never met anyone with such distinct features and colouring. As this Celtic warrior leaned towards Henio and breathed heavily, the suffocating stench of whisky enveloped the soldier who turned his head away, screwing up his nose and said, 'Excuse me pliz. I no vont trouble.'

'Eh, Hamish, did ye hear that my boy?' continued the large Celt, still fixing his gaze on Henio but speaking to his short, dark side kick. 'The Pole says he doesn't want any trouble. Who said anything about trouble, eh?'

The shorter one smirked. 'We just want to make yer acquaintance Polish laddie', he quipped.

Meanwhile, we had been watching the proceedings from our table and when the two hefty looking men barged in front of our friend, the four of us immediately got up to go to his aid. As we crossed the room, I noticed that the two village stalwarts who had greeted us and had been conversing with others of about the same age, had stopped talking and were watching the enfolding scene intently.

The warrior and Hamish glanced over at us. Hamish said drily, 'Oh look Robbie, the cavalry's arrived' and they began to chuckle as we stood solidly behind Henio, who attempted to get through to the two troublemakers. 'Wot iz de problem?' he asked, beginning to feel a little flustered.

Robbie spoke.' Look Pole, we don't want ye near our lasses. Do ye understand now? NO LASSES.'

Henio looked confused. 'Lasses? Vot are lasses? I see film called 'Lassie'.' The two men were about to reply to this, when the dark haired girl suddenly stood up with her friend, looking more annoyed than scared, her cornflour blue eyes blazing. 'How dare ye, Robbie McFee! We are not YOUR girls. We speak to who we like and if ye say anything more, I'll be having a wee word with yer mam and dad, so I will.'

The large Scot looked shocked.' But Hannah, you canna mean that, my wee lassie…'

'How many times, I am NOT yer lassie!' She too turned away in disgust from the stinking breath in her face, holding her hand up to her nose. She looked at her friend, who was too nervous to speak. 'Come on Sara, let's get some fresh air.' They picked up their small, white evening bags, pushed past the two protagonists and made their way to the door.

Henio had been impressed with the feisty young Scottish girl's spirit and followed her and Sara outside. We thought it best to keep an eye on him so decided to join them. Robbie and Hamish stood red faced, feeling humiliated in front of their village friends. 'We're nay going to let them get away with that, are we Robbie?' asked Hamish, looking expectantly at his friend, who was fuming.

The large Scotsman stared in front of him, eyes glazed, tight lipped. 'Methinks these Poles need teaching a lesson, Hamish. Are ye game fer it laddie?'

Hamish grinned. 'Och aye, Robbie. I'm game.' With that, they both went over to the bar counter where they had left their drinks, finished them in one drunken gulp, wiped their mouths on their sleeves and strode in the direction of the entrance.

The two village elders exchanged worried looks. 'I think it might be wise to call the bobbies Mrs. Andrews', said the Councillor.

'Aye, Mr. Stewart, I agree, ' and she hurried through the fire exit door at the back of the hall to the phone box outside.

In the meantime, Henio, the girls and ourselves had been greeted by the sight of Peter and Wojtek play wrestling on the little grassy area just in front of the village hall; the latter clasping his paws gently around Peter, who was laughing out loud. 'Hey lads, have you got our beers?' he gasped as Wojtek released his grip. He saw the two girls with us, smoothed down his greased down hair and dusted himself off.

' Hello. I am so plizd to meet you,' he said. The two young ladies retreated towards the door at first, staring apprehensively at Wojtek, but Peter tried to reassure them saying, 'Oh no, Wojtek okay. He no hurt you. Look.' Right on cue, Wojtek, delighted at female company, flirtatiously did his usual act of peeking from behind his paws, before rolling on the floor. The girls fell under his spell. 'Aah, isn't he sweet?' said Hannah, impressed.

The charmer then stood on his hind legs and started turning round, as if dancing to the uplifting Polka being played by our Company musicians. Bolek took him by his paws and they swayed together in time to the music, whilst the rest of us clapped to the beat and cheered them on. Wojtek loved dancing. The girls visibly relaxed and joined in with the clapping, giggling. Henio stood by

Hannah and Sara, whilst Peter sat with the rest of us on the ground, enjoying Wojtek's performance.

The two young women had heard of Wojtek and his antics and were thrilled to have the chance to see him at close quarters. They laughed and applauded every time he did a turn, which encouraged him to continue, making the most of being in the spotlight. 'He's *gorgeous,*' gushed Hannah. Sara nodded. 'I've head so much about the bear. What's his name again?'

Just then, a loud voice boomed in the doorway, 'Hey, Pole. I want to talk to ye!' We all turned round. Robbie and Hamish stood with arms folded, legs apart, like 'bad' cowboys in an old Western film demanding a confrontation. At almost exactly the same time, the music stopped, meaning that what was being said could be heard audibly by everyone inside. A number of couples stopped what they were doing and voicing 'Fight!' as one, made for the door to see the showdown.

Mrs. Andrews had just returned from calling the police and rushed over breathlessly to Mr. Stewart. 'They'll be here in a wee jiffy', she panted.

'And it won't be a minute too soon,' commented the councillor anxiously. With that, they and the other older patrons went to see if there was anything they could do to prevent a fracas.

The two troublemakers worse for drink, especially hefty looking Robbie, had strode out and made their threats as we stood in front of Wojtek who was still holding onto Bolek and thus momentarily hidden from view. As Mr. Stewart appeared behind Robbie and Hamish, he just managed to start, 'Now look boys,....', when Bolek let go of Wojtek's paws and we moved out of the way, revealing our enormous friend standing stretched to full height on his hind legs.

Robbie and Hamish stood motionless, eyes wide, mouths open in shock. They had forgotten about Wojtek, thinking that when he left the hall with Peter earlier, he must have gone straight back to the camp. 'R..Robbie.. do ye s..s..see w..w..what I s..s..see?' Hamish stuttered.

His friend spoke quietly and firmly without taking his eyes off our bear.

'Of course I see what ye see. D'ye think I'm an idiot man?'

'What are we going to do Robbie?' asked Hamish in mouse like tones.

Large amounts of alcohol having dulled any fear or reason, encouraged Robbie to stand up straight, then start to stride towards Henio announcing in a loud voice, 'Och aye Hamish, everyone knows the bear's tame. He'll nay bother me. I'll sort the hairy critter out!'

'But Robbie,...' began Hamish, not moving. He had consumed less whisky than his friend and so was more aware of possible danger. All at once, Wojtek bared his fangs and growled; quietly at first, then louder as Robbie began to walk towards them. Our loyal, protective bear had sensed a bad atmosphere and his sharp animal instinct detected aggression in the form of the large, angry Scot now walking purposefully towards them. Peter, Irek, Bolek and I exchanged knowing looks and as one stood up, Peter laying his hand on Wojtek's collar, ready to restrain him. 'No, kip avay,' warned Peter.

Unfortunately Robbie, deep under alcoholic influence, foolishly snarled back at Wojtek, resulting in the bear breaking free from Peter's hold, dropping onto all fours and making for the drunken hulk, who promptly fainted. Wojtek stood tall again over the unconscious troublemaker, though without touching a hair on his head.

Then in a victorious gesture, he opened his mouth and emitted another loud growl, but this time without snarling, just waving his paws.

Hamish was too scared to check on his friend, but the crowd from the dance hall cheered Wojtek and sang' For he's a jolly good fellow'. Wojtek feeling very pleased with himself and gratified at the applause he received, performed a little dance in front of the admiring crowd. Someone handed Peter a bottle of beer and he promptly gave it to Wojtek who downed the contents in one, then as usual, threw the bottle behind him just missing Hamish as we shouted 'Duck!' to the utter amazement of the villagers.

Robbie's shocked accomplice and another acquaintance of theirs, took this opportunity to quickly lift Robbie out of the way and into the foyer, where they laid him across a couple of chairs to sober up.

Precisely at the same time the police arrived on the scene, looking in consternation at the huge brown bear dancing to some lively music, whilst someone was being carried inside the hall. Sgt. Connelly took his policeman's helmet off and scratched his head in disbelief. 'What the ......?' he began, standing next to Mr. Stewart.

'It's alright Sergeant, I can explain,' started the councillor, who was rather fed up with Robbie and Hamish's penchant for creating problems at social events.

'I think you'd better sir,' said the policeman, who had been torn away from his weekly bridge game and so was not in the best of moods. '*This* story I can't wait to hear!' With that, they both went inside.

That was how Henio met his future wife.

* * *

CHAPTER 16

Attitudes

Even though our Polish army had fought valiantly with the British and other Allies, somehow once the war was over and we had lived here for a while, attitudes towards us for some reason seemed to change.

Many people were still kindly disposed towards us, especially in Berwickshire and we forged a close bond with the residents here (I'm sure Wojtek helped!) but there was a festering unfriendliness generally which reared its ugly head openly more and more often in other parts of the country.

These people complained about our presence in Britain and tried to persuade the government to quickly repatriate us, even though Winston Churchill had previously made a speech in which he acknowledged Poland's vital contribution to the war and that her 'exiles' should be given U.K citizenship. Incredibly, many British people actually believed that *we* were the problem, not Stalin! They wanted us to be sent back to Poland as soon as possible. This antagonism continued in other unpleasant ways for years afterwards too. For those of us who stayed in this country after we were demobbed, it was very difficult for example in the early 50's when we eventually left our 'Polish Person's Displacement Camps' to buy our own homes.

It was not uncommon to see signs with 'No Poles; no

Irish; no Blacks' attached to 'For Sale' signs. It seems unimaginable in the current politically correct climate and added to the hardship suffered by so many Poles (and others) who had been deemed good enough to help the Allies during the war, but not now to make a home here. We were prepared to work hard and honestly, so we really didn't understand what the problem was.

Actually, what jobs most of us did get were usually manual and very poorly paid but with long hours, though some who had the opportunity, went on to higher education here. We survived by being resourceful, frugal and with the love of our families that lived with us; we cared for and helped each other. It was impossible to return to our homeland, so we tried to make a life for ourselves here as best we could. Thousands more emigrated to other countries for their new beginnings.

We still didn't know all the atrocities Stalin was subjecting our dear country to, but more information of suffering and persecution had filtered through and we worried about our families that were still in Poland. Many letters delivered to our camp were full of hope and optimism at the prospect of eventually being reunited, but others contained terrible news of relatives and friends, injured, killed or missing. Those that came from Poland had been censored by the Russians.

As he had done all that time ago in the desert, when Tadek had got upset about his letter, Wojtek's heart now went out to any of our Company who received distressing news. He knew. As demonstrated on several occasions, Wojtek was very intuitive and in such cases would simply come and sit his bulky, warm, cuddly body next to whoever needed him.

Some of our soldiers believed British assurances that

Stalin was arranging democratic elections in Poland and so returned, only to frequently be shot as traitors. After a while, Stalin's true motives and actions were made public in the west, so soldiers were no longer under constant pressure to go back, though the remaining Poles here still had to fight their case politically to be allowed to stay in Britain.

So it was that a resettlement programme was launched to assess firstly what language and practical skills we had and also where we would live. After being demobbed, the government would move us to various resettlement camps for 'displaced persons' (basically groups of Nissan huts dotted all over the countryside) which would eventually include other family members who would be joining us. My own family would sail in from Africa on the *SS. Georgiu* in the summer of 1948. My brother Wladziu in the Polish Cadets would also be joining us. Our family unit would be complete and living in Seighford, Staffordshire, except for Bolek, who would stay in Liverpool. My brothers, sisters and I would find some local employment and so interacting with our British hosts, learn the language more, whilst the camp would be our family and cultural home for a few years, until a while after we married.

As we waited for political machinations to resolve all the official administrative and political issues, we did our best to counteract the frustrated monotony that was setting in at the camp. We would do our chores and help out the locals wherever we were needed. What lovely people lived near Winfield. We were very lucky to have them as our neighbours and they will always be a part of our lives.

Sometimes, we would put on a 'show' for them with Wojtek, either pretending to wrestle with him, or several of us pulling on one end of a long, sturdy rope, with Wojtek pulling on the other to the shouts of encouragement from adults and children alike. Unsurprisingly, Wojtek would win, though not without much strenuous effort on our part. When we fell like dominoes one after the other and Wojtek held the end of the rope in the air, like a victory trophy, someone would ask Peter if they could give Wojtek a beer or cigarette. Children gawped as they watched him swallow the lit cigarettes whole, their parents always careful to remind them that what he was doing was BANNED for them; that they should never try it because it was dangerous for humans.

This went on for months, until we were finally told that we would be demobbed. This was it. The real end of the war for us. We would become civilians like everyone else, except not like everyone else. We all wondered how we would adapt to life outside Winfield and in addition, it was the first time in years that we would be separated from many of our brothers in the camp. What we had gone through together forged emotional and spiritual ties that would never be broken.

We were contemplating this, when Irek turned to me, Bolek and Peter and said what the rest of us hadn't the heart to say out loud and what Peter had been worrying about internally for ages; 'What will happen to Wojtek?'

* * *

CHAPTER 17

Demobbed and in a dilemma about Wojtek

There was much heated discussion about Wojtek's future, some of us being realistic and saying that it was impossible for Wojtek to go to Poland, as the likelihood was that he would be shot by the Russians.

This would be practically inevitable if they discovered his role in the war with our Company. The last thing Stalin would allow would be a 'hero soldier bear' for dissatisfied Poles forced to live under his thumb and who might be just ready and waiting for an example of courage and strength against adversity to test their mettle against his communist regime.

Other soldiers however, seemed to look at the situation very naively and kept insisting that Stalin would keep his word and allow the democratic elections to take place. Why they still claimed this after all the publicised evidence to the contrary, I really didn't know. Perhaps they were so desperate to see their families in Poland again, they simply chose to ignore the facts before them.

Meanwhile, our camp at Winfield was now also being used as a temporary base for demobilised Polish servicemen until they left for a new life elsewhere as civilians. Large numbers of them came and went.

We all exchanged stories and they too fell in love with Wojtek who still lived with us. Peter was beside himself with worry about his charge. He couldn't imagine life without Wojtek, or how his beloved bear would cope without him. What could be done about him though? It was impossible to take Wojtek with him, wherever he moved.

Finally one day, our commanding officer Major Chelkowski had a quiet, private chat with the Lance Corporal. Wojtek was tethered outside asleep and Peter was cleaning his regulation black army boots, as the Major knocked quietly on the door. When Peter saw it was his distinguished visitor, he immediately guessed why he had come. He had been dreading this conversation.

'Look Peter, I know you're anxious about Wojtek. It's something we've avoided discussing for so long, but you know that we'll all have to leave Winfield ourselves soon. I don't mean to upset you Peter, but you know that you won't be allowed to take Wojtek with you.' Peter's heart stopped. He slowly placed his shiny boots on the newspaper sheet spread out on the floor and sat in his chair without a word, staring at the ground.

The Major continued in hushed tones.' I'm sorry Peter, but we need to think about his future as well as yours and to make sure that he will be well looked after.' He paused, looking at Wojtek's guardian, who was still sitting in silence, but now with his head bowed.

The Major took a deep breath and continued, but had to look elsewhere. He moved over to the window, focussing on the old birch tree outside.

'To that effect Peter, with the help of a lady who is a member of the Scottish/Polish Society, I have made enquiries with the officials at Edinburgh Zoo and they are willing to have Wojtek there.' He turned round to see Peter's reaction, but the latter sat motionless, speechless, his head in his hands. The Major was finding this very difficult. He was a kind man and felt a protective responsibility towards his soldiers. He was also fond of them and realising the strong bond that existed between his men, wondered how they would cope with being split as a unit. Peter and Wojtek were a separate dilemma. They really had become 'surrogate mother and child' over several years and the Major couldn't imagine how either would cope with separation.

He had felt great trepidation about this morning's meeting with Peter. The C.O went up to Wojtek's 'Mother Bear' and placed a hand on his shoulder. 'Look Peter, I don't want to do this, but I really cannot think of any other way of ensuring Wojtek's safety and well being. You are aware of what is happening back home. We could not send him there.' Peter looked up, white faced. His voice was almost a whisper. 'It's okay Major, I understand. I know you have always done your best for all of us including Wojtek. But what if they decide to move him somewhere else? What if we won't know where that will be? How will I know if Wojtek is alright?' His voice was trembling with emotion.

The C.O straightened his back and said decisively, 'That will not be a problem Peter, I promise you. I give you my word of honour. I too am very fond of our bear and wanted to guarantee as happy and secure a future for him as I could. Therefore I only agreed for the zoo to take Wojtek under very strict terms and conditions, meaning that they had to agree to his never being transferred from that zoo, unless I myself gave permission for this to happen. In other words, Wojtek will have a home there for life. The people at the zoo will look after him well, don't worry. You can be assured of that Peter.'

'Thank you Major,' said Peter, with difficulty. 'On my

behalf and Wojtek's, I thank you for all you have done for us.' He stood up to salute his senior officer and the C.O responded in a similar fashion. Suddenly, he took Peter's hand and shook it vigorously, saying as he did so, 'Thank *you and Wojtek* for everything. Good luck to both of you Peter.'

With that, he strode out of the door of the hut and sighed deeply before walking back to his own quarters with a heavy heart.

Feeling numb and in need of some fresh air, Peter went outside too and stared at Wojtek, who was still sleeping, oblivious to his fate. Peter's eyes filled with tears as he knelt down to stroke him. As he did so, Wojtek stirred and seeing Peter crouching over him, turned round and gave him a long, loving lick on his face.

* * *

CHAPTER 18

Goodbye Wojtek

I think that day will be imprinted on our minds forever. Even now, I can hardly bring myself to write about it. On that bitterly cold morning of 15th. November 1947, the saddest day in the history of 22nd. Company (Artillery) 3522, Wojtek left our camp and our Company forever. His life would never be the same again and neither would Peter's, or ours either for that matter. I stood with my brother, also Stas, Henio, Irek and Tadek as our dear bear came out of his and Peter's hut for the last time and happily bounded to the waiting truck. His eyes shone with excitement. We could hardly bear to watch, knowing his destination.

He was blissfully unaware of where he was really going with the 'mother' he loved so much, probably assuming he was going out somewhere for the day with him, as they often went on short trips together. Wojtek obediently climbed onto the back of the open truck. Peter wasn't driving, as he was standing next to Wojtek as usual for his safety. Another soldier Jan, was there to help him.

As the engine started, we all gave a dignified, respectful salute and waved them off. As the truck drove off into the distance, I'm not ashamed to say that I cried. And I wasn't the only one. There was a dark cloud hanging over the camp all day, with hardly anyone speaking and we couldn't eat. Apart from being upset about Wojtek, we all felt so guilty picturing Wojtek's joyful, trusting face as he sat at the back of the truck. I felt awful, like every one of us had betrayed him. How Peter would cope when he got to the zoo we could only imagine. We prayed for him and Wojtek.

Peter suffered for the whole journey. All the way there, he felt sick. He hardly noticed the cold wind blowing on his face on top of the truck and couldn't speak to either Wojtek or the friend who had come with them. Instead, he just stroked his 'child's' back with one hand, whilst holding one of his old blankets which would serve as Wojtek's comforter, tightly in the other. Memories of Wojtek flashed persistently, painfully through his mind, tormenting his spirit; happily meeting Wojtek for the first time as a vulnerable little bear cub; comforting him when he was small and scared, or injured; Wojtek growing up into a huge, gentle, adult, giant of a bear, getting up to all sorts of pranks that sometimes caused worry or frustration, but most often raucous laughter. Then Peter remembered Wojtek's memorable, historic contribution to the terrible battle in Monte Cassino. His adjustment to life in Scotland and Winfield also filled the soldier's thoughts, until all at once, he realised that they were in Edinburgh itself.

The journey took them down famous Princes Street with its imposing, old buildings, hardly noticed by Peter. Wojtek smiled at the incredulous looks he received from passers by, lapping up the attention. He felt like a star on stage again.

Once they reached the zoo, Peter and the other soldier were dismayed to find that they and Wojtek were being greeted by a number of people waiting with restraining equipment just in case, as they had never met Wojtek. Fortunately, none of the frightening looking instruments needed to be used, once they saw how docile Wojtek was walking on all fours in between Peter and Jan.

Peter felt numb as he alone unwillingly led trusting Wojtek into the enclosure surrounded by bars; his new 'home', though it felt more like a prison. Don't get me wrong, the zoo had done their best to give him a good sized area in which to live, but this after all, would be the only place he would be allowed to move around in. It would feel so restrictive after the freedom and space our dear bear had been used to.

Peter looked round for somewhere to put the blanket and just placed it on the ground. That blanket bearing his 'mother's' scent would be Wojtek's last physical link with Peter.

Peter enveloped Wojtek in one long, final hug and Wojtek in return licked his face. It was almost too much for the soldier. His heart was bursting, his head thumping. He had to keep swallowing hard so as not to cry out loud in his distress. Wojtek sensed that his 'mother' was a bit quiet and sad, but at the moment was still elated, thinking this was some new great adventure and turning round, went off to explore. Peter took this opportunity to make his exit and somehow forced himself to leave the enclosure.

He walked out of the gate and up to Jan waiting on the other side, with tears rolling down his cheeks. Jan was also crying. The pain felt by both was indescribable. Peter of course in particular felt the most upset and added to that, had to endure terrible pangs of guilt. He was leaving his 'child' behind on his own in a totally alien environment and he wasn't able to make his charge understand *why* he had to do it.

How would Wojtek cope without him? Would he be looked after with love? Would they hug him; groom him;

feed him his favourite snacks? How would he know if Wojtek really was taken care of properly? How would Wojtek feel when he realised that Peter would not be returning for him later? How would Wojtek cope when he felt lonely? Would anyone comfort him?

As he shut the gate and started to walk away, Peter's mind was bombarded with these thoughts. He tried to comfort himself with the thought that maybe one day he would somehow return to his 'child', but at present that didn't really cheer him as he had no definite plan in mind and anyway, these emotionally charged moments in the zoo were so heart wrenching that he couldn't really concentrate on anything else. Then something made Peter do what he promised himself he wouldn't. He looked back.

Wojtek had heard the gate close and saw Peter and Jan walking away slowly. Where were they going? Peter never left without him. Wojtek, feeling uneasy, tore over to the bars of the enclosure on all fours, stood on his hind legs and wrapped his paws round the cold bars, just as Peter turned round.

The two stared at each other for a few seconds, before Peter somehow forced himself to shout 'Wojtek, I love you!' Wojtek looked at him, confused and continued watching in dismay as the two soldiers walked away into the distance, wondering where they were going without him. He began to growl. When would they return and take him back to camp? After all, he had never had any reason not to trust Peter. He calmed down a little. He was sure Peter would be back. His mother wouldn't leave him here on his own. Wojtek went and sat next to Peter's old blanket. He held it tightly in his paws, absorbing the soldier's familiar scent and waited. Wojtek would be waiting for a long time.

Peter's friend Jan, who was also upset at leaving Wojtek behind, had the added trauma of watching his friend's distress. Peter had been very brave for a long time so as not to upset Wojtek, but once they reached the truck, his simmering grief erupted. He burst into tears and cried pitifully all the way back to Winfield, heart wrenching sobs shaking his broad shoulders, hardly able to catch his breath; his head buzzing, eyes swollen.

Jan wept too, both friends very aware of the empty space on the truck where Wojtek had been and where they wished he was now. To add to the gloom, daylight was already fading and freezing air pervaded their heavy army overcoats. There was a desolate feeling all around.

When they arrived at the camp sometime later and the C.O saw their distress, he asked to see them straightaway. We never found out what he said to them that afternoon.

Poor Peter was inconsolable. He wept every night for weeks after that and we all became very concerned about his health. He hardly ate anything and found it hard to get to sleep, images of Wojtek haunting him in the lonely darkness of long, quiet nights; or dreams about his Wojtek alone in the zoo enclosure making him wake in a cold sweat, heart pounding.

We agreed between ourselves not to talk about Wojtek in front of Peter, as the least mention of his 'child's name would upset him. His conscience was tormented at leaving Wojtek behind, though he didn't really have any other option. He constantly worried about Wojtek's welfare. He pined for him and was convinced that Wojtek was suffering in the same way also alone in his accommodation, wondering why his 'mother' hadn't come to take him home. Peter was heartbroken. He tried to comfort himself with the thought that his Wojtek was safe and that once he (Peter) himself was settled, they would hopefully meet again. The bond between Peter and his 'surrogate son' was so strong, that his yearning for the beloved bear became a part of his life for the rest of his days. The sadness about Wojtek never left the soldier.

Sometime later, Peter did settle in London and was happily reunited with his wife and child. Then it seemed that he could go and visit his dear charge at the zoo, as he had promised himself on departing Wojtek's enclosure that dreadful, dreary November day. However, after much soul searching, Peter had to acknowledge with great regret and sadness, that it would have been too painful for both of them to meet for the first time in ages just fleetingly and then say goodbye again. It wouldn't be fair to Wojtek. Peter loved him too much to put him through that again. Besides, he wasn't sure how he himself would cope with a temporary, doubtless very emotional reunion before bidding him farewell once more. His heart had not recovered from the time he had left Wojtek. And it never really would.

* * *

CHAPTER 19

Where is Peter?

That first evening, Wojtek ate the snack that had been left out for him and once in a while went and stood at the bars of the enclosure, wondering where Peter was and straining to see into the distance.

It was getting hard to see further out, as it was getting dark. Wojtek began to get worried. Peter had never left him for this long on his own before. It was lonely and smelt strange, unfamiliar. He clung onto the Peter's old blanket, absorbing the smell and for a while felt a little comforted. Peter would return. Sometime later, Wojtek couldn't keep his eyes open any longer and going into his 'house' shelter inside the enclosure, fell asleep.

When he awoke the following morning, he was confused at first not to be in his hut at Winfield. Then he remembered where he was and panicking, went outside looking for his cherished guardian. Still no sign of Peter.

Wojtek went over to the gates where Peter and Jan had stood the day before and was worried not to see them anywhere. Where were they? When was Peter coming back for him? He suddenly felt alarmed. What if the impossible happened and Peter *didn't* come back? As the day wore on, Wojtek became increasingly anxious. He paced the enclosure, growling and whining, frightening the zoo staff, although they comprehended why he was on edge and did their best to reassure him. But that didn't really help though they spoke kindly, because it was in English, not in his language, Polish. Someone braved the enclosure to leave Wojtek his dinner, but the distressed bear wouldn't touch anything.

Wojtek was very intelligent and after an extremely long day of disappointed waiting for Peter, as another evening approached, he realised that Peter was really not returning this time. The unthinkable had happened. His 'mother' had gone. He was left on his own. He wasn't going back home on the truck. Wojtek was distraught.

He felt angry first of all, then hurt and confused. How could Peter have left him like that? Why, what had he done? He'd been on his best behaviour all the way here and going into his 'prison'. Peter loved him, so why did he leave him in this strange place with people he didn't know and couldn't understand? They seemed kind enough, but they were strangers. He wanted his mother. He stood on his hind legs and snarled, then howled pitifully and so loudly that it resounded throughout the whole zoo.

* * *

CHAPTER 20

Wojtek adapts to his new home

Although the transition had been extremely traumatic for all concerned, Edinburgh Zoo in fact turned out to be an ideal choice of new home for Wojtek. Over the years, this large institution had earned a reputable name for itself and was not only renowned for looking after the animals under its care well and sensitively, but also catering for their emotional needs; that is, providing an immediate environment that would be familiar to their species and where they would be happy and flourish. Today, the zoo is firmly established as part of Edinburgh and is to expand even more.

The lifestyle that Wojtek was left to experience was indeed a very fortunate one in many ways, but it's also worth remembering that the animals who lived there enjoying such privileged treatment were often frustrated; their freedom now being tremendously restricted compared to what it once was and in addition they had to suffer being taken away from much loved family and friends.

The zoo director, Mr. Gillespie, had a good heart and wanted the best for the animals under his care. He kept a watchful eye on his new 'guest'. He knew Wojtek was clever and sensitive and had been told by the C.O some time ago of the extraordinarily special bond between the bear and Lance Corporal Prendys.

Wojtek's sadness was tangible. The staff at the zoo, also kind, conscientious workers, had informed their chief of Wojtek's reluctance to eat and how despondently he either sat in his enclosure for long periods at a time, or would occasionally wander over to the bars, looking through them sorrowfully, still hoping for Peter's reappearance on the other side of them. This sad sight pulled at everyone's heartstrings.

So the wise, compassionate director did two things. Firstly, he would go to see Wojtek daily and spend some time talking to him to cheer him up and gain his trust. The former although well meaning, would have succeeded more in its objective if it had been in Polish; the latter made more difficult after Peter's failure to show. Still, Mr. Gillespie persisted, intent on making Wojtek feel more at ease. He even provided a little pool for him to use to help him adjust, having also been told of Wojtek's passion for water and swimming. Still Wojtek was depressed. He kept puzzling over why Peter had left him here on his own for so long.

This prompted the director to write to Major Chelkowski in confidence, describing Wojtek's unhappiness and difficulty in settling in and asking if the soldiers from our Company would like to visit him soon. Inevitably, the offer was eagerly accepted by many of us at Winfield, though for reasons I have already explained, Peter couldn't bring himself to go.

In the first few weeks, those that did see Wojtek would be careful what they said about him in front of Peter afterwards, keeping their comments brief and positive. There was a part of Peter that was desperate for information about Wojtek's progress behind bars, but it was very difficult for him to actually listen to comments from the men on their return to camp. The rest of us suspected things might not be very rosy when some of them wouldn't look Peter in the eye.

When Bolek, Stas, Irek, Henio and I decided to drive up to the zoo one bright but raw morning ourselves soon after the first two contingents of visitors had been, we understood why.

Arriving at Wojtek's enclosure, we were shocked to see our loveable, lively bear sat morosely on his own, listless; his once clean, shiny fur looking dirty and matted. Peter wasn't there to groom him. The area behind bars, Wojtek's new 'home' looked acceptable enough for an indifferent, curious day tripper, but to us it was heartbreaking. Poor Wojtek. How must he be feeling imprisoned there day after day with no chance of any change of scenery or being able to roam the countryside; miles away from his family and not understanding why. My heart went out to him. Warm rays of sunshine warmed our backs as we stood there, every so often shivering as icy gusts of wind breathed over us.

It was early, so there were hardly any visitors yet. In fact, there was only us and a young family there at the time, a couple probably in their thirties, both dark haired and dressed in warm winter clothes. Their daughter, a pretty little blonde about nine years old, was talking to her mother whilst opening a sweet wrapper. Wojtek was focussing his attention on the small piece of confectionary and hadn't really noticed us yet. In unison we called out 'Wojtek! Jak sie masz?' ('How are you') in Polish and Wojtek's head turned towards us straightaway in joyful recognition. My heart jumped as well.

He was ecstatic to hear words in his own language and from familiar faces and so upon seeing us at the bars where he had longingly stood day after day for his Peter, leapt over to where we were waving frantically and stood on his hind legs holding onto the bars. Close up, Wojtek looked even more unkempt and he looked like he might have lost a little weight, but now at least he was his usual lively self and his eyes shone with joy. He grinned and uttered familiar contented noises. The little girl on the other side of the enclosure with her parents shrieked in delight. Her parents smiled; the father took his old Box Brownie and pointed it at us, clicking away.

We managed to get the lengths of our arms through the bars, stroking Wojtek's head, ears and chest. How we had missed him! He rubbed himself against our hands and licked them affectionately. Stas pulled a brown paper bag out of his coat pocket.

'Look Wojtek, I've brought you a tasty honey sandwich from my breakfast rations. I wanted *you* to have it'. He took it out of the bag and pushed it in between the bars, pulling his hand away quickly as Wojtek grabbed it and stuffed it into his mouth. He demolished it in one and licked his lips, sniffing near Stas for more.

'Eh, Wojtek', called Henio, lighting a cigarette, 'Remember these? Do you fancy one mate?' and threw it over the bars. Wojtek dexterous as ever, picked it up off the floor, put it into his mouth and swallowed it in one. The couple with their young child gasped and clapped. 'Would you mind if we joined you?' shouted the father. We shook our heads. 'No, no. Pliz, come here wit us. You very velcome,' yelled Irek.

The amiable family joined our little group, but kept a little distance from the bars. They studied our uniforms. 'Polish?' asked the woman. We nodded in affirmation.

The little girl was staring at Wojtek's insignia on

Henio's shirt sleeve. 'What's that?' she queried. Henio glanced down and saw the object of her curiosity. 'Ah, zat is Wojtek.' She looked puzzled. Henio elaborated. 'Zis,' he said slowly, pointing to the symbol of Wojtek carrying the shell, 'iz Wojtek,' turning towards our bear at the bars. The girl and her parents were flabbergasted.

'You mean....*this bear,*' began the mother looking at Wojtek, 'is the same as *this bear?*' Wojtek just sat staring at us, hoping for more treats and wondering when he would be allowed out to play. Why was he still on that side of the bars and why hadn't Peter come?

'Yes, answered Bolek. 'Wojtek our bear. He hero in var. He helps us in Monte Cassino. He...how you say... ..he carry ze shells.' The father let out a low whistle. 'Is that really true?' he asked stunned.

Henio stood up straight and said in a dignified manner, 'Yes, of course. He is soldier like us. He understand Polish, not English', wagging his finger, and....' he paused for effect, 'he drink ze beer and like cigarette!'

'Wow,' breathed the little girl.

'I canna believe my ears Georgie,' said the woman, astounded. All at once, the little girl took another sweet out of her navy coat pocket and pushed it through the bars. It dropped on the concrete.

'Annabel! No!' her horrified mother shouted. 'He might not like sweets and it's still got the wrapper on. He might choke!'

Henio chortled, 'No, no, iz okay. He eat *anyting!* Wojtek alvays hungry! Whilst they were discussing his dietary habits, Wojtek picked the sweet up rapturously and rammed it into his mouth, complete with wrapper.

'Can I take another photograph of the bear? What was his name again?' inquired Georgie.

'WOJTEK! we all said loudly in unison. Wojtek knew it was a photo opportunity and acted accordingly. He stood on his hind legs, grinned and waved his paws. We gestured for the man's wife and daughter to stand on either side of Wojtek (on our side of the bars), whilst we leaned in or knelt down to be part of the picture. We all posed smilingly, including Wojtek. 'Say cheese!' called Georgie and we all obliged, Wojtek opening his wide mouth, his pink tongue hanging out.

Henio lit another cigarette and threw it to Wojtek, who promptly shoved it into his mouth as always and swallowed it. The family just stared in wonder with their mouths open. We chuckled and started to explain our bear's dietary habits.

All this time, we hadn't been paying much attention to the zoo keeper's assistant, unobtrusively cleaning out Wojtek's small shelter, but simultaneously keeping an eye on the proceedings with interest; all the time moving closer on the pretext of brushing some grass to one side of the enclosed area. He was an older man in his sixties I'd say, dressed in a white shirt, brown corduroy trousers and a blue overall. His salt and pepper hair was largely covered by a brown, flat cap.

Stunned by the sight of Wojtek gulping down a lit cigarette, he decided to fetch the director. Swiftly but quietly, he let himself out of the rear exit and closed the gate behind him. Then he dashed in the direction of the main office past more compounds, when he ran into the director himself.

'Mr...Mr...Gillespie,' he panted, hardly able to catch his breath.

The director looked at his employee with concern. 'Mr. McTavish, slow down sir. Watch yer blood pressure.

What on earth is the matter man?' McTavish composed himself. 'Ach. Mr. Gillespie, ye must come at once sir. It's Wojtek....'

The director felt alarmed. 'What's the matter with Wojtek? What's happened?' He began to walk very quickly towards our bear's enclosure.

McTavish couldn't talk and run, so he just accompanied his boss to Wojtek's den. On arriving at the rear exit, Mr. Gillespie halted at the sight in front of him, his worried employee close behind. Carried away by the moment, Henio had dared Irek to climb over the bars and have a mock wrestling match, just like we used to, with Wojtek.

McTavish stared in horror. 'Oh no! We must get that soldier out of there! Let me get....' and he moved to open the gate. To his surprise, his boss put his arm out in front of him. 'Nay McTavish. Wojtek won't hurt him. I've heard of this, but it's the first time we're witnessing it. Watch.'

'But no-one's allowed in there sir. It's dangerous. The bear could get vicious and hurt the laddie.'

But Mr. Gillespie was adamant. 'I said no Mctavish. They'll be alright. Just watch.'

McTavish still felt uncomfortable, but did what his superior ordered and stood ready to intercede at the slightest doubt of the bear's intentions, eyeing the bristly broom in the corner of the enclosure, next to the 'DO NOT FEED OR TOUCH' sign. No-one thought to add '*Or climb into the enclosure to wrestle with the bear*'. If he hadn't witnessed it with his own eyes, he wouldn't have believed it.

Irek and Wojtek meantime, were enjoying their wrestling bout. By this time a bigger crowd of astounded onlookers had gathered, watching and pointing as the bear held Irek in an arm lock. The soldier laughed and extracted himself from Wojtek's firm but gentle grasp.

The crowd applauded and Wojtek finding himself the centre of attention again, readily obliged and performed the customary roll on his back with his legs in the air, then stood up again and waved at his audience. Adults and children alike shrieked at his antics. Without taking his eyes of the jovial scene, Mr. Gillespie spoke softly. 'See, McTavish. This is what Wojtek is really like; a sensitive, intelligent showman who loves his soldier friends with the love of a human being. Everything the Major told me about this bear is true.'

McTavish whispered in awe, 'A bear like no other I've ever seen.'

'That's right McTavish, this is a historic time for our zoo. I canna believe there is another bear like this *anywhere* in the world. He's starting to show us his real personality and what a personality it is.'

They continued watching as Irek jumped over the bars and Henio lighting another cigarette, threw it over to Wojtek, who once again swallowed it without hesitation. On seeing this fascinating feat, the large number of people now encircling the area hushed, staring in stunned disbelief.

McTavish suddenly recalled why he had run off to find the director in the first place. 'That's what I was trying to tell you Mr. Gillespie,' he said.

The zoo director did look quite perturbed at first, but when he saw that Wojtek seemed to be suffering no ill effects from his 'trick', instead grinning and walking on his hind legs around the enclosure facing the adoring crowd, he relaxed.

'Next time, we'll bring you some beer Wojtek!' called Bolek and we all laughed. McTavish thought he must be in some kind of strange dream. 'Mr. Gillespie, did he say beer?'

'Yes, McTavish, I believe that's another of the pleasures he enjoyed whilst a Private in the army.'

'Did you say *Private* sir?'

Mr. Gillespie smiled at the zoo keeper's assistant's astonishment and put his arm round his shoulders. 'McTavish, there's a lot more to this bear than meets the eye. You can't imagine what he's been up to during the war- and afterwards. He's a real hero. One of these days we'll have a wee chat and I'll tell you all about it.'

Just as they started walking away and some of the crowd dispersed, we realised with sadness that it was time to return to Winfield. The fun had come to an end, temporarily at least. We called to Wojtek, blew kisses and waved.'See you soon Wojtek!'

'Love you!'

'We'll bring you more cigarettes and beer don't worry Wojtek!' we called out in turn, as we turned round to make our way to the truck. My heart felt heavy and I tried to hold back the tears as Wojtek rushed over to where we had been standing, all at once experiencing that same feeling of alarm as when Peter had left. It seemed such a long time ago. And Peter hadn't come back. Why were we going now ? Why weren't we taking him with us? Why did he have to stay here?

That frightening feeling of abandonment enveloped him. His hurt and frustration turned to anger. He ran there and back along the length of the bars opposite where we were standing, then stood on his hind legs by the iron railings as we very reluctantly walked away. He roared so loudly and howled in such a tormented way, that two zoo keepers who had been working nearby rushed to see what was happening.

It was indescribably painful leaving Wojtek like that. The other soldiers should have warned us. Unless that is, they thought someone might let Wojtek's state of mind and behaviour slip in front of Peter. We too would have to be careful not to upset our friend with any of these heartbreaking details.

The zoo authorities had meant well and we also had the best intentions for Wojtek, but maybe this wasn't such a good idea after all if it firstly excited Wojtek and made him feel overjoyed, then he had to watch us all disappear again for goodness knows how long. It was extremely painful and confusing for him and difficult for us too. How Peter must have felt on leaving his 'son' here, I could hardly imagine. It wasn't surprising he was in such a state. They were both suffering greatly.

We made our way down the path slowly with heavy hearts and tear stained cheeks, no one really in the mood to speak. Wojtek's cries followed us all the way to the truck.

* * *

CHAPTER 21

Wojtek finally accepts his new home

It took the best part of a year for Wojtek to accept that when his friends from Winfield came, much as he loved their visits, that's all they were and that he wouldn't be getting a ride back to the camp with them; to the open fields and sweet, fresh Border air. He finally realised that he would have to accept, albeit reluctantly, this as his new home.

But he still held out the hope that one day his 'mother' would come back for him. For many months to come, sometime during the day, he would wander to the place by his enclosure where Peter had said his emotional goodbyes and linger for a while, straining to see into the distance. Was that his voice he could hear? When there was no sign of him, that was probably the loneliest time and Wojtek would become downcast for a while, retreating into his shelter for a few hours.

His keepers felt pity for the friendly bear. Over the months they had learnt of his experiences in the war and at Winfield and felt quite privileged to be looking after such an extraordinary creature. They also slowly learnt his habits and became accustomed to his ways, as he did to theirs. Gradually, they formed a bond with each other and Wojtek's inherently sociable, exuberant personality bounced back to some extent. The keepers for their part, would spend time talking with him and frequently provide tasty snacks which cheered him up.

By the time all of us at Winfield had been demobbed, many of the men were still making regular trips to see our wonderful brother who was sorely missed, until some of us moved to resettlement camps south of the border. Bolek and I couldn't face going back to the zoo again after that time we saw Wojtek and then had to leave him on his own, crying so pitifully.

We heard that when our comrades visited him, he wrestled and played with them as usual and the director of the zoo, good man that he was, asked his staff to turn a blind eye to any Polish soldiers jumping into the enclosure to have a friendly tussle with Wojtek, or giving him the odd cigarette or bottle of beer.

Now when his friends left him at the end of their visits, our bear no longer dashed to the bars near the gate trying to go with them. We were relieved for his sake that he seemed more settled in that way, though whilst we were still at Winfield, I often imagined him following us out of the zoo and climbing onto the truck, to freedom. It was upsetting to think he would be stuck in there for the rest of his life, regardless of how marvellous the place itself was.

In a way, our bear's situation was a symbol of ours. He was forced to 'live in exile' at the zoo, away from what had become his home with us. Although his new habitat was safe and comfortable, it wasn't his real home and spiritually never would be. Similarly, we were safer in Britain than we would have been in the mother country and under the circumstances, quite comfortable. However, our real home was Poland and we yearned to return to a free homeland. That wouldn't be possible for a great many years and by then we would have established families here of our own, with roots for the next generation firmly planted. Still, we would reminisce about our homeland and memories we had from before the war, for the rest of our lives.

Scottish people learnt how to pronounce Wojtek's name and some other Polish words and greatly enjoyed our bear's enthusiastic response when they called out to him in his language. He particularly loved children visiting and would amuse them and their parents by walking on his hind legs, then all of a sudden roll over on his back as was his habit. His reward was usually a treat thrown over to him.

Some of the children from the villages near Winfield used to visit Wojtek with their families. He recognised them and when they called out his name in Polish, would wave in their direction. Their parents would sometimes throw him a cigarette; lit of course.

For the time being, Wojtek tried to fill his time in other ways, including swimming in his pool, but it would only provide temporary satisfaction. He longed to be held by Peter and groomed daily by him. It used to feel so good being cleaned and brushed, especially with the love he had from Peter. He missed that human contact and besides, it stopped his skin from feeling too itchy. There weren't even any sticks for him to scratch himself with and there was still no Peter.

At the end of the day and after polishing off his generous dinner, Wojtek would retire to his shelter, alone. Just before he fell asleep was the loneliest time, when silence reigned over the zoo, except for the animal noises from his fellow inmates and at times like this, he felt overwhelmed by memories. Then during the night, he often dreamt of Peter stroking his fur in that loving, soothing way he used to.

Wojtek was like a veteran performer of the human sort; putting on a fine, entertaining show to a very appreciative audience during the day, then acquiring a different, quieter persona when everyone had gone home. I think winters must have been the most testing for him, with shorter days, meaning less visitors and long, dark nights.

Mr. Gillespie felt sorry for Wojtek and so he had the idea of bringing a couple of other bears to play with him in his pound for company. This thoughtful gesture didn't really have the desired effect on our bear. He liked playing with them, but they were just bears and acted purely like one would expect of their kind; a pleasant, but not very exciting experience for Wojtek, who had always regarded himself as 'one of the lads' and missed the sort of human interaction with which he had grown up. I'm sure he would have appreciated the well meant gesture, but it probably just served to remind him even more of what - and who - he'd left behind. Thus he still appeared quite downcast at times.

Bolek and I moved down to Seighford Camp in the Midlands, where we were joined by the rest of our family, including my brother Wladziu, who was also shipped over with the Polish Cadets and as it happened, my future brother - in - law, Gienek. Bolek would eventually go to Liverpool, where he would remain.

The rest of our Company scattered far and wide; many staying in England, but others trying their fortunes abroad in a new country. Times were very hard for all of us. We hardly had any grasp of English and no money. Fortunately, there was plenty of work after the war.

We kept in touch with Henio, Irek and Stas for the rest of our lives. You don't experience what we did together and then just forget about people. It's impossible. Those that remained in Scotland and lived close enough, visited Wojtek as frequently as they could during his stay there and word filtered back to the rest of us as to the state of his health and happiness.

Our bear had learnt to cope in this zoo environment, punctuated by moments of fun, play and snacks, but his heart was spiritually always with Peter and his time with us; from a lucky, very young bear cub sold to us unsuspecting Polish soldiers by that little boy (I wonder what happened to him?) to growing up with our Company in the stifling heat of the Middle Eastern deserts; witnessing the horrors of battle at Monte Cassino whilst helping us carry out our duties; then playing, dancing, swimming, chasing the 'field wildlife'(rabbits, foxes, birds) in picturesque, peacetime Winfield.

As time marched relentlessly forwards, Wojtek's condition slowly deteriorated. When he reached old age, he wasn't too keen on performing much anymore. He felt stiff, his joints ached and so he preferred the warmth and cosiness of his comfortable bed and heat lamp in his shelter, to which he had now become accustomed. I think it's fair to say that even though the zoo looked after Wojtek in an excellent fashion, being parted from his human brothers but most of all from his dear Peter caused Wojtek emotional suffering to the extent that he never really got over it; he simply coped with it as best he could once he realised that his circumstances wouldn't alter.

We heard with much sadness, that Wojtek died on 15th. November, 1963.

He was 22. Even now, I find myself thinking of the significance of that number for our beautiful hero, his having of course been a very important member of our 22nd Company, Artillery.

I wept all day on hearing the news through a letter from Henio, who had married Hannah and was living in a suburb of Edinburgh with her and their four children. We had only seen them once since we moved to London. What increased my sense of grief, was that my brother Bolek, a vital part of these cherished memories, had become ill and died soon after he moved to Liverpool.

I call to mind how at the time, with a heavy heart, I pulled out my old army insignia of Wojtek carrying a shell. Young, brave, comical, energetic Wojtek and then…… ..sad Wojtek behind bars in the zoo, trapped in a safe, comfortable, but lonely prison where he would end his days. Our Company brothers united as one for such a long time, then those that survived the war had mostly scattered to different parts of the country or world. The war had seemed never ending and yet the past twenty years or so had gone in a flash.

I could hardly bear it and my caring wife Krystyna who I'd married in 1951 and was the mother of our two young sons, Jurek and Rysiek, comforted me for hours as I cried like a baby. Finally, emotionally exhausted, I dried my tears, deciding that from now on, I would focus on the good times and be grateful for those; for my precious brother and wonderful friends, including a very special one, Wojtek.

* * *

CHAPTER 22

The Sands of Time

That was forty seven years ago, nearly half a century! I recollect the days when I was a young man during the war and we used to think that someone aged thirty was old! Now my own children are a lot older than that and Krystyna and I will soon be *great* grandparents.

Jurek our oldest and his wife are expecting their third grandchild any time now back in London. *Grandchild!* It doesn't seem that long ago that Jurek was in short trousers himself! Now we're to be *great grandparents* again! How can that be? I feel like a museum piece at times.

Our youngest son Rysiek is also married with three (adult) children and a grandchild. They all live fairly close to us in south east London, where Krystyna and I moved to from Seighford just after we married nearly sixty years ago. The rest of my family, apart from Bolek, stayed in the Midlands.

I became a founder member of the Polish Club in our area, where we army veterans and our families would meet up regularly and still do when our health will allow. Many such associations sprang up all over the British Isles; wherever the Polish families had resettled after the war.

These weren't 'closed' to everyone other than Poles by any means. Wherever you live, you have to integrate for the good of society as a whole, though there is no harm in keeping and nurturing your own identity and culture within that society (in fact it is important to do so) though without trying to enforce it over and above that of the host country. Added to that, is the need to learn the language of the country in which you live, part of the process of integration. I believe it is also essential to share and explain one's beliefs and cultures with others in order to promote better understanding and therefore tolerance. In my personal opinion, these are vital and achievable objectives for a truly successful multicultural society.

Our English friends, including local V.I.P's, have also always been invited to social events; in fact at our club for example, an Anglo-Polish Society was formed many years ago which used to meet there regularly, its members enjoying a Polish beer or glass of wine in the bar downstairs after monthly meetings. Our restaurant and continental food shop have also always been popular with Polish, English, Irish and Italians alike; quite cosmopolitan!

However, our shared experiences have unified us in a unique way and we never want to lose that. Nowadays, British ex pats living in their own little communities abroad with bars named and decorated patriotically might comprehend our feelings to some extent, though they *chose* to settle far away from the country of their birth; we didn't. It is much more than sentimentalism that binds us so tightly.

Hence we, our wives and children have worked together from the beginning to encourage our language and culture; to teach the next generations their roots and how it affects their lives in this country. To ensure a good grounding in the religion and history of our country, these subjects (and the former) were and still are taught in

Polish Saturday schools. The Parish priest is regarded very highly, as the clergy always have been in Poland by its people and he plays a pivotal role in the Polish community.

I should add though, that we were also determined to ensure the best possible education for our children, in the hope that would make life easier for them when they were older; help them obtain good, well paid jobs so that they wouldn't have to struggle like we did.

Consequently, to help our youngsters integrate into British society and progress more rapidly at school, the majority of us taught them to speak and write at least their names and letters from the alphabet in English before they started Primary education and ensure they took their studies seriously.

They already spoke and were reading very basic textbooks in Polish and coped very well on the whole in having to master another language at almost the same time. Being bi lingual helped many of them go on to study Languages and most others either went to institutes of higher education obtaining degrees, or worked well at other chosen forms of employment straight from school. They've had the unusual, but we believe for them very beneficial experience, of two different lives successfully merging; the one within their families and Polish communities and the other playing, working and socialising with their English friends.

We are so proud at having been able to raise the money ourselves for our clubs and churches. Many was the time we stood on street corners in all weathers rattling tins, asking for donations. That and any money we could spare from mostly meagre wages were the sacrifices we made to build our Polish communities. It's so hard to imagine that was nearly sixty years ago, but our clubs are generally still thriving, though in this depressing time of recession it can be more difficult to raise the necessary funds for essential maintenance and repair work. Many of our generation and older are no longer here and a significant number of our children have either moved away or just don't come as regularly as they used to, resulting in a smaller income to fund these 'home from homes.'

More than twenty years after the historic fall of communism in Poland and when the fist influx of young Poles came over a few years ago, we were delighted that they would help, support and replenish our clubs with more members, so we greeted them warmly. Remembering how hard things were for us, we have tried to give them whatever help we could.

We love our kinfolk but overall our clubs don't appear to have the same significance for them, which I suppose is only to be expected under the circumstances. We do feel the obvious, inherent connections of sharing the same country of birth, language, religion and artistic culture, but apart from that, our actual life experiences are totally alien to each other. The Poland we remembered and that they knew from childhood and now represented, are totally different. They are here entirely of their own volition and hardly aware of what caused the older patron's enforced exodus from their country and what our clubs mean to us.

Since Stalin's communist regime imposed itself on our country after the war, so few Poles returned home to relate our experiences and many of those who did so openly, were shot or imprisoned in labour camps. In addition, there was such strict censorship that our story was hardly made known. How I wish these younger native Poles understood what we went through.

Our club is very close to the Catholic Church we once shared with the English, Irish and Italians and still has a large congregation today, as do others in different parts of the U.K. In fact, it is an oft mentioned irony in British papers nowadays, that they have helped to keep *most* British parishes alive, halting the general decline in numbers.

Young people, make the most of your beautiful, idealistic, optimistic youth; for before you know it your body will become old; your views cynical and your dreams could be distant rainbows. Chase and catch them while you can.

My life turned out different to anything I could ever have imagined. I think everyone I know from our country who experienced the trauma of being torn from it by force feels the same, yet we feel so blessed to have come through all that and for what we have now. You might think it strange after all these years to speak of Poland as 'our country', but that is where we are from and proud of it. We didn't choose to be taken from it and it was impossible to return. We will always be grateful for the chance to make our home in Britain and have done our best to fit in, though it hasn't always been easy, for reasons I have already explained.

Fortunately, times change. Attitudes became more tolerant. For our part, we did our best to mix. Our English is now much improved, though we still speak with a distinct Polish accent. Actually, having been away from our mother country for so long, our vocabulary is not as extensive as it once was in our native tongue. As a result, our children and grandchildren find it amusing to hear us speak in 'Polish English' sometimes, with the odd Polish word mid-sentence frequently being replaced with an English equivalent.

'Emil! It's time to go!' Krystyna's voice broke into my thoughts.

'Okay Krys, I'll just fix my tie'. I paused in front of the mirror for a few seconds to look at my reflection. Not so bad for an old one, if I do say it myself. My hair might be grey, but there's still quite a thatch of it and I've only put on a few pounds. It's strange. I feel like a young man trapped inside the ageing body of a pensioner.

'Don't forget your coat! It feels freezing cold here in Scotland after coming up from London. I'm glad I brought my warm boots and hat as well, ' my wife called from the bedroom.

I walked to where she was standing at a slower, more sedate pace than I used to and gazed at my precious wife waiting for me in the doorway. Her once lovely, shoulder length, fair hair now had quite a lot of grey in it and had been cut into a neat, shorter style that really suited her. I stood there for a few seconds gazing at her, lost in thought.

'Penny for them?' she asked laughingly.

'You look lovely.'

'Thank you my handsome Polish soldier. You don't look so bad yourself; very smart in that suit. Are we meeting the others there?'

'Yes and Henio has invited us all back to his for some bigos and a few beers for old times sake later. I'm sure there'll be lots of food at the reception, but nothing beats good old Polish bigos.'

'They might provide that there as well you know. The Scottish/Polish Society are very well organised.'

'I know my dear, but you can never get enough bigos!' I patted my stomach with a grin. 'Besides, I want to see Henio's house. Do you realise, we've never actually been there yet after all these years?' My thoughts turned to another friend, someone dear to us all that we wouldn't be seeing today.

'I wish Peter could be here today. I can't believe he's been dead for forty two years. Sometimes it feels like just yesterday that we met up with him every Sunday at our club, yet he's been gone for so long. I still miss him as well you know. And as for Bolek......' The words suddenly stuck in my throat.

Krys held me close. 'I know dear, I know you miss both of them, but remember, they're part of the reason for the ceremony today. They're being honoured as well as Wojtek. My dear Emil, I know this is hard for all you soldiers today. That's why we wives are here! Someone's got to look after you!' She was sympathetic but practical. Best choice of wife I could have made.

I gave her a kiss, took a deep breath and announced assertively, 'You're right. We're doing this for them, all of them. It's important they're remembered and that maybe after this, a large part of Poland's history as yet untold and unknown by much of the world for so long will come to light.'

'That's it Emil. Stay strong. By the way darling, did you say that Irek and Ania, Stas and Paula are staying at our hotel as well?' inquired my wife.

'Well Irek and Ania are driving up from Birmingham this morning, as they stayed there last night, though how he can manage that long drive in one day I don't know. Mind you, there are representatives from Polish clubs all over coming up here today; many of them travelling long distances, though I suppose they *are* coming by coach. As for Stas and Paula- I know they live just down the road from here in Berwickshire, near where our old camp was, but they fancied treating themselves to a night at this hotel and as we're here anyway……'

'Oh, I see, 'said Krys wryly, 'and you're thinking of having a few nightcaps after Henio's…'

I put my arms round my perceptive wife and said 'We haven't seen each other for so long dear and you can have a good chat with the girls.'

'*Girls*? Have you had a drink already dear? At our age we're flattered to be called '*mature ladies*'.

'You know you look great for your age my darling.'

She smiled. 'Flatterer. ' All at once she sounded awkward.' Er..just out of interest Emil…are you men going to the zoo where Wojtek was? I thought…..' She stopped and I know it was because of the expression on my face. 'I'm sorry Emil, I shouldn't have brought the subject up.'

'No, no, it's fine Krys, but we're not going there because…well…we just couldn't. ' My voice faltered. I looked directly into her eyes. 'Do you understand what I mean dear?'

Krys looked straight back at me and said softly, 'I love you.'

'I love you too. Now lets get a move on Krys, we're supposed to be at the ceremony at 11. It's already 10 30. Fortunately, our hotel is only around the corner from the monument; it should only take us a few minutes to walk there and it's one of the best hotels in Edinburgh I've brought you to, you know darling,' I quipped, trying to lighten the mood as we left our room sensibly wrapped up for the bitter cold, with heavy, warm coats, hats and gloves.

'And I'm married to one of the finest soldiers,' said Krys, linking her arm through mine as we walked down the long corridor and down to the main entrance, 'Though

I think it might take us a bit longer to walk there than you think Emil, 'she continued flippantly, giving me a knowing look. 'After all, we aren't spring chickens anymore my dear.'

'I know Krys, but we can pretend for a day can't we? ' As the chilly air hit us outside, I felt for the small plastic bag in my coat pocket. It was still there. Something to remember you by, my dear Wojtek.

* * *

CHAPTER 23

Honouring Ours

It feels like we've come full circle. It had been a bright but bitterly cold autumn day in November over sixty years ago when we had visited Wojtek that time at Edinburgh Zoo. The first time my 'gang' and I had ever walked away from him. How difficult that was, but how even more painful it was for our wonderful bear; a free spirit trapped in the equivalent of a gilded cage. You were beautiful, clever and unusual. You really did have the heart of a man and a brave one at that.

As I stare at his and Peter's bronze images, my eyes become blurred with tears. I picture young Wojtek's smiling face coming alive in my mind as Peter kneels beside him, stroking him gently that first time we met him on that dusty road in Persia. I like to think that you've been reunited now, up there, never to be separated again. I wish you were both here in real life, not just as statues, impressive as they are. I wish Bolek was here too. Perhaps he is up there with you. How I miss you all.

I take out the little package wrapped in a plastic bag from my coat pocket. I pull off the outer bag and extract a brown bottle of beer. All of a sudden, I hear the crisp crunching of dry, sharp leaves behind me.

I turn round to see my dear wife and old comrades with their wives standing in a little group. They smile warmly.

'I thought you'd all gone to the reception with the others', I start to say in surprise, as Krys comes up and puts her arm through mine.

'We were', she said, 'but we didn't want to leave you on your own here. Not today.' I am still holding the beer bottle in my hand. Krys notices, but doesn't mention it.

The rest of them slowly approach us. Henio still smiling, says, 'I hope you weren't going to do that without us,' He glances at the bottle adding, 'because we all had the same idea.' With that, the other wives take a bottle each from their large handbags and hand them to their spouses.

The eight of us form a circle around Wojtek and Peter. Suddenly, we're enveloped by glorious, golden rays of sunshine and as we old soldiers raise our bottles to the peaceful, cloudless, bright blue sky above, they glint in the radiant light. 'To our brothers', we announce loudly as one.

* * *